THE WAKE

KYLE S. BERKLEY

Published By:
Cheryl Barton Publishing, LLC
P.O. Box 962
Reisterstown, Maryland 21136
www.crbarton.com

For permission requests, write to the publisher, addressed "Attention: Permissions Coordinator," at the address below.

Cheryl Barton Publishing, LLC
P.O. Box 962
Reisterstown, Maryland 21136

Ordering Information:
Quantity sales and special discounts are available on quantity purchases by corporations, associations, and others. For details, contact the publisher at the address above.

Orders by U.S. trade bookstores and wholesalers. Please contact prez@crbarton.com

Book Cover Artwork by: Stacie Doi

Dedication

In loving memory of my father, Samuel Berkley.

Acknowledgements

This book is dedicated to the memories of Robert Bowman, Kenneth Bowman, Collette Burns, Antonio "Bones" Washington and Chris Burton.

I'd like to thank God for providing me the vision to write this story and for having experiences that led to the overall story.

I would like to thank my wife, Rebecca, my daughters, Savannah and Sage, my sisters, Kyrissa, Toi, Kim and Brenda and my parents, Samuel and Betty Berkley for being a constant inspiration to me.

I would like to thank the men I'm blessed to call my brothers, Angelo, Lamont, Andre, Durant II, Anthony, Mike and Nelson. Thank you to my pastor and co-pastor Randy and Grace Spann, my friends Cathy, Ellie, Patrice (panda), Nichelle L. and Christina. I would love to thank Nichelle B., Dr. Brown, Dr. Carr, Traci and Lawanda for putting up with my craziness. Of course, before I continue, I have to give thanks to my Aunt Cella, Uncle John, Aunt Jean, Uncle Tom, Uncle Elosha, John-Mark, Jenell, Ron Jr, Jamilaah Brittney, Alex, Evan, Jeremy, Ashley, Lesha, Charles Jr & Charles Sr, Charmeda, Reggie and all my other cousins, aunts and uncles. A huge thank you to Michael Reilly and my R Dash family, Poe, Rasheed, Deezil and Corey. We made history together for many years. A big thank you to Stacie Doi for the book cover artwork and design.

I would also like to thank everyone who lends their support of the *4Us Initiative* as we provide services to Baltimore's at-risk population. I know that I may have forgotten some names, please forgive me.

Kyle

Table of Contents

An Introduction to The Wake

In, *The Wake*, the Bradley Funeral Home is a community resource created by Allen Bradley, with the assistance of the Ridgley Square community leader, Pastor Donald Avery. Prior to its opening, Allen had experienced several run-ins with the police and found a passion for gardening while working at the Baltimore City Pre-Release Unit. Following Allen's last discharge from the Maryland Department of Corrections, he received an internship at the Jacobs Funeral Home. After the death of Simon Jacobs and the closing of that funeral home, Allen had a goal of servicing the Ridgley Square community with the opening of his own funeral home. Since the opening, he witnessed a growing number of challenges, such as; violent crime, vacant homes, decreased employment opportunities and a lack of homeownership. He was also dealing with a new community development program that aimed to remove all current residents and business owners.

On a warmer than normal December day, the seven viewing rooms at the funeral home are packed to capacity with news crews, police, family members, friends and people involved in the Ridgely Square community. Understanding that the obituary can only tell a highlighted portion of a person's life, Allen believed that only those impacted can provide the full story of the person that is being viewed.

Having a love for flowers, he named each viewing room after a different flower with the philosophy that they were plucked from the garden after they bloomed perfectly. Each viewing room has its own story and the flower that bloomed is one of many that are waiting to blossom in their own time.

The writing of this novel was done to provide a mindset of complicated grief, family secrets and gentrification in an urban environment. Each chapter was designed to tell a different story, but as the novel goes on, you realize that the stories are intertwined. To give the stories life, I pulled from a lot of real life experiences and situations that currently plague the City of Baltimore. Hopefully, the reading of this novel will provide insight, create questions and generate meaningful discussions. I pray you enjoy this novel and I look forward to the discussions this will bring.

Proceeds from every book sold will go towards the *4 Us Initiative*, which is a not-for-profit that provides transitional housing to homeless mothers and children in need, victims of sex trafficking and survivors of domestic abuse along with recreation and preventive care to inner city youth. Thank you for taking the time to purchase and read this novel.

God bless!

1
THE GARDENIA CHAPEL

December 16, 2016

"The flowers are beautiful," a faint whisper says inside of the funeral home chapel filled with large wreaths and floral arrangements. The beautiful, intimate sized chapel, a place of prayer and worship, came complete with twenty-six pews, thirteen on each side, a shiny black grand piano to the right of the pulpit, and California Vinyl wood floors that were shined to have a pristine appearance for onlookers. The Gardenia Chapel is one of the largest viewing rooms in the Bradley Funeral Home, the only funeral home in the Ridgely Square community located in Baltimore City.

On any other day, Florence Simms would have been placed in a larger viewing room due to the size of her family, but on this beautiful December day, all seven rooms within the funeral home are occupied with others who have also been laid to rest.

Along with the Gardenia Chapel, the funeral home is comprised of six additional viewing rooms named after flowers, that include; the Poinsettia Chapel, the Protea Viewing Room, the Calla Chapel, the Monte

Cassino Chapel and the Iris Chapel.

"Look at that," the whispering voice says regarding the rose-colored coffin containing the elderly Florence Simms, who though older, was heavier than most. She looked beautiful in her white dress, a contrast to her dark skin. Her age was apparent due to the silvery color of her full head of hair that peaked out around the edges of the custom-made white church hat adorned with a gold bow. Slightly to the left of her still body sat a pair of wire framed glasses she was known to wear frequently. They were noticeable due to the small light fixture that cast a glow over her frame. A note written by her daughter, Linda Gibbons, rested underneath her crossed hands which were placed atop a small white Bible.

"I'm glad she picked my communion dress," the voice said admiring the white dress. For years she had worried about her daughter's sound judgement and capabilities to maintain the stability of the family.

"I wish our old church had those pews," the voice said admiring the funeral home's Gardenia Chapel room.

Florence Simms had served in the capacity of trustee, evangelist and mother at her church, New Hope Greater Love, until the church closed its doors due to complications with funding. She and the pastor, Donald Avery, tirelessly worked with other community leaders with the hopes that they could prevent community reconstruction that would hurt the church where declining membership left financial constraints and a lot of confused and worried people.

"I wish they would have had the funeral at the church, but this will do," the whispering voice said as the smell of fresh carnations filled the air.

A bright glow from the sun shined bright into the chapel through the large bay windows that lined one wall of the viewing room as three Bradley Funeral Home staff members walked in wearing black suits, white shirts and black ties, a staple attire for them. Two went to stand on opposite sides of the chapel serving as ushers for the visitors who would soon enter. The third went to stand patiently next to the coffin while glancing at his watch. They were ready to begin.

April 16, 2016

Florence Simms, also known as Mother Simms, a mid-seventy-year-old woman with skin that was as dark as the midnight sky, a contrast to her white as snow, silvery hair, sat stoically inside of Pastor Donald Avery's tiny office inside of the New Hope Greater Love Church, frustrated at how their conversation was playing out. She looked at the pastor giving him a once over and taking note of his balding head with little signs of hair here and there. His thin frame was covered in a coffee-stained, lint covered brown suit that had seen better days. She often admired African American men, but his attire was giving them a tainted presence.

"Having this man come in is not a good idea. We are tapped out on the building fund and you want to have Dr. Hakeem Andrews come in here and preach? We can't afford to throw money way. You know Titan Industries is trying to buy everything over here," she said concerned about the direction the New Hope Greater Love Church was headed in.

Her mind drifted to Titan Industries, a company whose purpose is to purchase property with the intent of developing new communities and most times, the community did prosper after their acquisition.

"Yes, and the last time I checked, I am still the pastor which makes this my call, Mother Simms. There will always be companies like Titan that will try to develop in our communities," he said.

A moment passed between them as they sat inside of the office with peeling beige paint covering all of the walls that had once been white. The floors were covered in stained carpet from years of wear and tear and very little cleaning. The office was decorated with pictures of Pastor Avery, his late wife Michelle and other church members, adding some semblance of beauty to an otherwise rundown space.

Michelle and Donald Avery met in high school but became close after he returned home from the Vietnam War. During his deployment to Vietnam, he developed an addiction to heroin which became prominent after his honorable discharge. Michelle had also developed an addiction to heroin after being drugged at a house party with former high school classmates. They began a long-term love affair mixed with substance abuse for years until Michelle started attending church with her best friend, Florence Simms. As Florence and Michelle began to grow in ministry, Donald began to attend church and their love for ministry helped impact their recovery.

Prominently displayed on those same walls sat Pastor Avery's degree from Howard University School of Divinity and a certificate from the Community Reach Substance Abuse Program where he worked as a counselor for a short period of time. The Program, which was created by several licensed mental health and substance abuse practitioners in the Ridgley Square community was later closed due to the lack of funding to keep it opened and operating.

"Pastor, with all due respect, I do not believe this is a good idea. We emptied the outreach money to help that boy, Allen Bradley, who can't get his life right. He's in and out of jail and you want to help him start a company?" she asked with disdain as she looked at the cluttered desk and turned her nose up at the pungent smell of mildew that wafted throughout the office. She wondered how anyone could work productively in such a dilapidated space.

"That's what the church does. We help people who are in need," the Pastor replied.

Mother Simms sighed with impatience.

"God helps those who can help themselves," she said sharply.

"Is that so?" Pastor Avery said, leaning back in his torn leather office chair.

Trying to prove her point even more, Mother Simms picked up a printout of the church's financial record and glanced at it before looking back toward the Pastor so that as she spoke, he could see and hear her angst.

"When we opened the doors to this church, you made me a Trustee. I'm thankful for that and to also serve in the capacity of church mother for some time now. I know you trust my judgement, so I'm asking you to listen to me on this, too. Having Dr. Andrews come here and preach is a bad idea," she inferred matter-of-factly

"Oh? Why is that?" Pastor Avery responded softly, trying to be open about an opinion other than his own. He and Mother Simms were long-time friends and as she stated, there was a level of trust between them.

"He charges thousands to minister," she replied.

"Thousands?" Pastor Avery questioned, not quite sure how she came up with the amount that Hakeem Andrews required for public speaking engagements. He was concerned that she had been misinformed. Relaxing in the chair and resting his arms on the desk, he leaned forward to listen more closely to discern from her information if he was incorrect or if she was.

"Yes, thousands and we don't have thousands to give him. We have needs that are not met here in our church and that would be a major expense. You gave that boy money for his business venture, which is like throwing cash down the toilet. The Dixon, Scott, Jordan and Michael families have all moved out of state. They were good, faithful members who paid tithes and offerings regularly."

Pastor Avery thought back over how he had helped pay for Allen Bradley to attend college and open up a funeral home a year ago without the consent of Mother Simms or other church members. Allen had two prior drug related incarcerations for possessing marijuana and an assault charge that he had helped get expunged from his record. He was still frustrated that Mother Simms had begun spreading rumors about the mismanagement of funds at the church on Allen's behalf which led to a division between him and several church members.

The Dixon and Jordan families were instrumental in helping the New Hope Greater Love Church build a substantial savings which provided the ability for them to purchase several homes in the Ridgley Square community. Mother Simms felt that the Dixon and Jordan families should have had a more prominent role in the church, other than the advisory council. As the head trustee, she had hoped that the Jordan and Dixon families could have provided support in her department, which came with a lot of growing responsibilities thanks to the new homes they had purchased.

The Scott family along with Pastor Avery and his wife were able to open a food pantry and emergency shelter, but those were lost due to a tax lien. In November 2015, the responsibility of trustee became too great for Mother Simms due to the lack of help and her advanced dementia when she failed to file the taxes or pay the water bill for the property. That allowed Titan Industries to purchase the property from the Baltimore City Mayor's Office.

The Jordan family advised Pastor Avery not to take out another mortgage on the church because it would create a new debt and when membership decreased, the Michael family reluctantly introduced Pastor Avery to Sage Realty, a local company that purchases homes and businesses from struggling owners and in return, allowed them to maintain the property through a rent-to-own program.

"What's your point?" he asked impatiently.

"They all had career jobs!" she yelled. "We may have one or two working families who are members with stable employment. Add to that perhaps ten members with unstable jobs they could lose at any time. Look at the economy in Baltimore City where everything is going under. We can't afford Dr. Andrews and looking at things, we can barely afford ourselves. Sage Reality has received an offer from Titan Industries and if we can't pay Sage, what will stop them from folding our lease and taking the deal that Titan is offering?" she asked.

"Hakeem Andrews is not a doctor; he's a minister. His father was a doctor and I'm not on salary, so there is money we are saving right there. I live off of the retirement from the steel mill where I worked for many years and I receive benefits from my time in military service. Sage Realty has a relationship with this community and I believe they are dedicated to that relationship."

Pastor Avery tried to relax back in his seat though inward, he was agitated by her concerns, but understood the seriousness of having Titan Industries come in and shaking things up. Along with Mother Simms, he was also invested in the Ridgley Square community as a leader and together, they have tried to maintain the community's culture.

Ridgely Square has had a rapid decrease in home ownership and access to fresh food, along with an increase in crime and vacant houses. Titan Industries has proposed to reconstruct the community with premium homes, schools and shopping centers. The concern is, in the past, they acquired properties and provided a complete makeover in communities by raising property values and making it unaffordable for middle-class African American families to move back and take up residence. The chief operators of Titan Industries were a brother and sister duo, Chandler and Chanel Titan, who had in the past, been followed around by a reality television crew who document people who took buyouts from them in exchange for their homes. The show was recently canceled when groups spoke out in protest that the show exploited minorities who live in impoverished communities.

"I get that pastor..."

"I don't think you do," he said cutting her off before she could complete her thought. "We have a job to do here. We will have ministries coming out of this church and it's up to us to give birth to those ministries. That means we have to find a way to bring in preachers like Hakeem Andrews. We need to move forward with having him here for the sake of our survival," he lamented and hoped they could put an end to the conversation. He wasn't so sure of that when he looked at her and saw discord on her face.

"You can't do that or we won't have a church. Please don't be foolish," she pleaded.

Mother Simms could tell that Pastor Avery wasn't going to back down and neither was she. She prepared herself to leave, saying what she came to say. She stood to leave and as she did, Pastor Avery took her by the hand and spoke in a calm, soothing voice.

"We are doing God's work here," he said standing and towering over her while he looked down in disappointment that she couldn't see his vision. "It might not seem perfect, but in time, it will all come together."

Seeing no need to continue fighting an uphill battle,

Mother Simms exited the office and the church.

May 11, 2016

As the sun began to set on a May evening in Baltimore City, many community leaders, business owners, home owners and renters from the Ridgley Square community are gathered in the Senior Care Nursing Home's community room, a meeting area where many politicians and organizers have met with community members in the past. Over the years, the room has kept an inviting appeal with paintings of local figures such as Thurgood Marshall, an American lawyer, serving as Associate Justice of the Supreme Court of the United States. He was the Court's first African-American justice. There was a painting of Victorine Adams, the first African-American woman to serve on the Baltimore City Council. Placed prominently beside them was a painting of Cab Calloway, an American jazz singer and bandleader who played the Cotton Club in Harlem, New York City and attended school in Baltimore at the Frederick Douglass High School.

The paintings added to the ambience of the brightly lit room with its clean, black and white tiled floors. In the air, there was the faint smell of pine as if someone had recently given the space a good cleaning. People were gathered in the space to hear the latest from Titan Industries' representatives, siblings, Chanel and Chandler.

"We have a plan to improve this district," Chanel

said glancing at everyone in the room which was filled to capacity. She used her eyes to scan from one side to the other as she tried to connect with each person she encountered. She knew those gathered wondered why they should even listen to her a tall, blonde-haired woman, coming into their community to tell them how to make their lives better. She only hoped they would listen to what she and her brother had to say

"My brother, Chandler, and I have seen this community go downhill with the murders, drug dealing, car thefts and the lack of community initiatives. We are hoping to help," she said and looked down the long table where they sat along with another couple known as the Littles, familiar to those in the community. She smiled as Chandler looked out over the crowd and began to speak.

"As my sister said, our company can help with those things that plague your community. What we are planning will enhance your lives, not hurt it."

Like his sister, Chandler saw the glimmers of discontent from community members looking on at him with his bleached blonde hair and professional presence, telling them how bad their lives were. He knew from their facial expressions that they were unhappy with his words, but he continued on, hoping to find a few allies in the crowd.

"We're prepared to offer most homeowners up to seventy thousand dollars today for their homes."

Before he could continue, he heard a murmur and

caught the glare of one woman in the crowd.

"No," Florence Simms said in anger as other homeowners looked on, some happy and others not so happy at the prospect of selling their homes. "From what I've heard, you want to build condominiums in this community after you knock down our homes and not many here would be able to afford to live here, forcing a lot of families to live elsewhere, perhaps in communities worse than this," she said. She was determined to not go down without a fight. She tried making her point to Pastor Avery and since that didn't work, she was hoping to share her concerns with those from Titan and others in the community.

"That is correct," Chanel said. "This community needs a fresh start and we can provide that."

Florence would not be swayed with her stern look of dissatisfaction.

"Why can't you provide that fresh start with us here? Some of us have had our properties for generations," she said, standing up to look around the room to see if anyone else agreed with her. Chanel quieted and allowed her brother to speak.

"Let's be honest. We see what's happening here. The schools here suck, there are no jobs and I don't see a future. The only way to improve this would be a complete makeover. You think putting a pretty pink bow on this community will make things better with the same people? No, I don't believe so," Chandler said in a relaxed, yet confident tone. He wasn't trying to be insulting to people who had lived their entire lives in the community, but he knew that he had to be honest with them.

"Then we won't sell our homes," Florence said. Before she could finish, a young man in the crowd stood and turned to her.

"Speak for yourself," he said says. "If I can get my daughter out to the county and get a place, that's fine with me."

"If they're going to rebuild where your house is now, the value of the property will be worth a lot more than seventy thousand," Florence countered. She looked around and saw that others didn't agree with her. She turned as Chanel cleared her throat to interject.

"No disrespect, but your houses aren't worth half of what we're offering. This is a come up and all you have to do is sign the contracts," Chanel said.

Everyone turned as Pastor Avery stood to speak.

"Other than the condos, what else are you building?" he asked. The pastor was hoping to keep the meeting from getting out of control by looking for the silver lining.

Chandler and Chanel looked between each other before responding.

"A sports complex, a small outdoor strip mall with restaurants and stores, office space, a new community college and a theater," Chandler replied.

"Then what will my church become?" Pastor Avery

asked. He'd heard Chandler mention a lot, but nowhere did he hear anything about the state of New Hope Greater Love Church.

"The plan for that space is a parking garage," Chanel added, while glancing at Pastor Avery and then at the expressions of others in the room. "We will make sure you will be compensated for the transition you will have to make moving from that property, Pastor Avery."

Murmurs filled the room as Pastor Avery sat down. He didn't hear what he expected to hear.

September 11, 2016

"Who will be helping me with the family reunion?" Florence asked her daughter Linda, as they sit at the kitchen table of Florence's row home on a warm September day. The home that had been purchased by her great-grandfather, Thaddeus Simms, a carpenter and preacher, has been a part of the Simms family for three generations. The kitchen table where they sat was handmade by Thaddeus himself.

Linda poured tea out of the pitcher while hungrily looking at the food spread out on the table. Her stomach had been growling and rumbling loudly for over an hour as she waited for her mother to finish cooking. Her excitement grew when she realized her mother had made macaroni and cheese and baked barbecue chicken wings. She couldn't wait to dig in knowing she was a great cook. It had been weeks since

Linda had a good home cooked meal without processed food, due to all of the fresh food markets in Ridgely Square moving miles away. The Simms family had relied on Pastor Avery to provide transportation to the supermarket in Baltimore County for the last few months when he was able and had free time. Florence's primary care physician encouraged her to change her diet because of her health problems with hypertension, strokes, diabetes and a diagnosis of Alzheimer's disease.

"Ma, no one offered help with the family reunion. Leon and his wife missed the reunion this year. Uncle Daddy and 'em said they couldn't make it up because of the hurricane. Aaron and the kids are at Fort Bragg with David for his graduation from basic training."

Aaron, Florence's first cousin, had distanced himself from the family after making partner at the investment firm where he has worked for the past ten years. He and his wife Tora focused their lives on their children, Patrick, David, Megan and Karen.

Leon, the youngest of Florence's three children and the only surviving male, moved to Arizona five years ago after getting into a fight with Linda's husband, Daryl. Linda and Leon had a brother, Laurence, who died during a robbery in June, a few months ago.

Uncle Daddy, born Samuel Simms, III is Florence's brother who lives in Rome, South Carolina where he isolated himself from Florence following a heated argument regarding Linda protecting her husband after he made an inappropriate gesture towards his daughter.

Aaron, another of Florence's brothers, recently retired from the Maryland Department of Corrections and moved into a trailer on Uncle Daddy's land in South Carolina. Aaron's son David, recently joined the United States Army. His twins Warren and Danielle are enrolled at Morris College, in Sumter, South Carolina. Aaron has expressed concerns in recent years to Florence about Daryl and has informed her that he will not allow Danielle to come around the family until Daryl has been arrested for what he did.

"Once again, I have to put the whole family reunion together myself," Florence said as Linda shook her head in disagreement. She was bothered that her mother didn't remember the reunion had already taken place. Florence's advancement of dementia has led to her forgetting family functions and regular activities. Linda sometimes forgets that her mother has Alzheimer's because of her ability to take care of herself and others.

"Ma, the family reunion was a couple months ago and the only people that came was us," Linda said softly hoping to jog her mother's memory.

Florence was startled as she realized she had forgotten what month they were in.

"Did anybody send anything to them beforehand?" she asked.

"I thought you were. Time got past us all. We will

do better next year," Linda said stopping in her tracks. She had to remember that her mother was battling Alzheimer's along with recovering from a recent stroke which was having an impact on her ability to think clearly and remember actual events. Looking at the sad look on her mother's face, Linda was overcome with a feeling of disappointment in herself, something she felt when her mother compared her to her other siblings.

"Did Tiffany come with all of her bastard children?" Florence asked.

Linda paused being caught off guard by her mother's off-the-cuff comment and tone. She was surprised to hear her make a reference to her own granddaughter in that way since she was fond of and close to her. Since her mother's stroke the month before, Linda's tone and feeling toward people had changed.

"No, ma'am. She's taking classes online to be a nurse. You know she's been going through it with her last baby father Keyon and her current boyfriend Tony."

"Does Tony live with her?" Florence murmured in a sarcastic manner.

"Yes, ma'am."

"She has no idea what Jesus was talking about when he said turn the other cheek. She just rolls over and shows both cheeks. Only thing she can do right is have ugly babies by a bunch of felons. Any of them rap or play basketball?" she asked.

"No, ma'am."

"Your daughter gets the laziest men and they can't even try to rap. Have you talked to Daryl?" she asked.

Linda thought about Daryl who had experienced sexual abuse from his uncle at an early age, which led to him questioning his sexuality. He began to develop different personalities throughout the course of his life, one being a childlike personality, which appears sweet and quiet spoken. The second personality is intelligent and opinionated. The third personality is impulsive, violent and sexually aggressive towards females. The fourth personality is blames others for the problems he has faced throughout the course of his life.

Daryl attempted to prove his masculinity, even getting involved with a gang called the Market Home Boys. The gang consisted of adolescents who lived in the now demolished old Ridgely Marketplace Homes, known for robberies, assaults and murders from 1975 until 1999 when the high rises were demolished. Daryl was nicknamed Cube in prison for selling large amounts of cocaine. Since the time of the first incarceration, he had been imprisonment for drug trafficking as well as three dismissed cases of sexual assault against teenagers in the west Baltimore City area. Florence knew that Daryl's recent incarceration was due to an infraction with her granddaughter, Tina, her now deceased son Laurence's daughter.

After his death, Linda agreed to take his Tina in until she finished high school. It didn't take long for Daryl's sexual predatory history to repeat itself, causing Tina to contact law enforcement.

Linda shook her head in dismay. Upset that out of all the things her mother could remember, she would recall her daughter's multiple children and her husband being locked up.

"I'm not talking to him, ma."

"You married him. I knew that man was a pervert. That's probably where Tiffany got her nastiness from. They going to take them kids from her. As hard as she tries, she can't get away from bad people. At least she in college and not in jail, like your husband," Florence said as she placed dinner rolls on her plate so that they could eat.

"Can we change the subject?" Linda asked not wanting to talk about her rapist husband. Her mother wasn't saying anything she didn't already know and all she wanted to do was eat.

"Yes, we can. I need help with the church's building fund. Can you put together a fundraiser for me?"

"Mom." Linda said thinking about how to remind her mother about what happened to the church. "Do you think we should focus on that now?"

"Well, there is something I will need you and Leon to look into," Florence said standing up and walking over to a wooden basket that contained several envelopes. "I need you both to continue paying the taxes on this house."

"Yes ma'am," Linda said thanking God that her mother forgot that it was already her responsibility. The taxes on the property have not been paid in quite some time. She didn't want to bring up the fact that she had been mismanaging her mother's funds since becoming her representative payee.

"I need you to make sure you do this Linda," Florence said shaking her head in disappointment. "We are terribly behind on the taxes and I don't want Daryl to have anything to do with this house or my money. It's a shame out of all the men you could marry, you had to marry a rapist."

"I didn't know he would be like that," Linda responded sadly that the conversation kept turning back to him.

"Ask Leon to help you if you can't handle it."

Florence placed more food on her plate and sat down to eat.

"I will." Linda wanted the entire conversation to be over with.

"If Leon doesn't help, ask Tiffany. She's good at using her brain when she not using other body parts," Florence laughed and began to eat.

December 8, 2016

The sounds of oxygen machines and hospital monitors saturate the atmosphere as Florence laid peacefully in her hospital bed at the Ridgely Square Hospital with her granddaughter, Tina standing close by.

"Thank you, grandma," Tina said. At seventeen, she was a thin, beautiful girl with a light brown skin tone. She stood sadly next to the bed while rubbing Florence's left hand knowing that this visit wasn't like previous visits. Florence's history of strokes and Alzheimer's had progressed and the medical staff informed them that she also has several blood clots that are surrounding her heart.

Sad while looking at her grandmother laying helpless in the bed, Tina thought back over all the times her grandmother was supportive after her own mother, Gina, had abandoned her and her father Laurence, who was no longer with them.

Gina, who had been married to Laurence, ended up developing an addiction to opioids after having surgery on her cervix. After the prescription was reduced and eventually expired, her addiction graduated to heroin. After years of stealing family valuables and leaving used syringes around the house, she finally abandoned her family all together.

Tina briefly looked out of the hospital room window at neighboring houses with snow covered yards and rooftops before feeling her grandmother's hand move. Fearful of touching the intravenous therapy line running into Florence's forearm, she backed away but stayed close.

"They said I have to stay in foster care," she explained. Tina had faced a recent share of hardships after the murder of her father and after being sexually assaulted by her Uncle Daryl. Her aunt Linda had also sold her father's house to cover her grandmother's medical expenses. She began to feel the weight of the world on her as she realized that the last two people she felt were really in her corner had been her grandmother and her cousin, Tiffany. The reality of her grandmother's health deteriorating didn't help her feel any excitement about her future.

"Just make sure you graduate sugar," Florence said faintly, not able to remember her granddaughter's name or what she is talking about. Feeling that she knows the young lady's face, she gives her a warm smile.

Tina began to cry as tears rolled down her cheeks while thinking about the blood clots surrounding her grandmother's heart. With that and everything else happening around her, she smiles briefly thinking of the strength her grandmother has always shown. Battling Alzheimer's and suffering from four strokes over the last two months, she continues to show signs of peace on her face.

The dim lit room has an odd silence to it, as the television plays reruns of game shows, along with the voices of medical staff in the hallway. Tina, wearing a denim jacket covering her arms, thinks of the loneliness she feels with her family. As the idea that no one really understands the problems and changes happening in her life, she daydreams of the vacation she and her father had years ago when they went to the French Open to watch Serena Williams compete.

As Florence looks off into the distance, Tina drifted out of the daydream and glanced at a plastic bag on the windowsill that was filled with small boxes and pill bottles. She placed her hand in the bag and pulled out a prescription bottle of OxyContin. Reading her grandmother's name on the bottle, she placed it inside of her own jacket pocket.

"Tina?" Florence forcefully yelled, startling her. "Is that you, where is Laurence?"

Shocked by her grandmother's call and wondering if she noticed her placing the pills inside of her pocket, she realizes that her grandmother is not fully aware of what's going on.

Thinking about her father while unable to answer and at a loss for words because her father had been murdered earlier in the year, she struggled with how sorrowful she felt that he was gone.

It had been her grandmother who had broken the news to her that he was gone. Unable to hold back the tears of her grandmother's limitations and realizing her own mortality, she walked toward the hospital room door where she was met by her cousin, Tiffany. They hug outside of the hospital room door as other medical personnel walk throughout the hallway. The subtle background sounds of beeping and muddled conversations fill the air as they talk.

"How have you been holding up?" Tiffany asked

her.

"I've been good, I just hate the house they have me at," she replied.

After being sexually attacked by Tiffany's father, her uncle Daryl, Tina now lived with a foster family until she graduates high school. "I wish I could stay with you and the kids," she added.

"I do too," Tiffany answered and looked away, feeling guilty that her father had sexually assaulted her. "I don't have the room in my apartment right now," she added.

"I understand completely," Tina said. "I wish that things could have been different."

Tiffany was about to respond when her cell phone vibrated in her pocket. She pulled out her iPhone with the cracked screen and after looking at it and not recognizing the number, she put it away. "That's the fifth time this person has called me," she sighed as the phone rang again. This time she did answer.

"Hello," she answered angrily. "This is Tiffany Gibbons."

She listened as an aggressive female voice asks for identification on the other end of the phone. She then listened, learning that her daughter Kenya and Kenya's father, Keyon have been involved in an accident and have been transported to the emergency room.

"I'm here at Ridgely Square Hospital now on the fourth floor, I'm coming down to you now," she said nervously.

"What's wrong?" Tina asked once she saw a look of concern on Tiffany's face.

"Keyon was involved in a hit in run and Kenya was with him. They are here in the emergency room. I got to go down there to check on her. If my mom comes back from the dining area, she is not allowed to make any decisions for grandma because I have power of attorney."

Wanting to tell Tiffany that she does not want to be around her mother after everything that happened but realizing the seriousness of Kenya being involved in an accident, she nodded in agreement and went back into the hospital room. Noticing the blank stare on her grandmother's face, Tina felt emotionally abandoned by Tiffany and her grandmother because they were the last two people in her corner.

2
THE ORCHID CHAPEL

December 16, 2016

"They came out for real," a teenage male voice whispered inside of the funeral home's larger sized chapel where music played in the background. Admiring the growing crowd in the chapel, the voice said, "Man this is serious." As the leader of the political activist group for African Americans, Justice 4 All, approaches the front of the chapel, several news crews begin to film. The voice says, "where is coach?" as the music stops.

November 17, 2016

"Can we do the Strong Easy?" Tyrone asked his coach.

Tyrone Clinton, a slim built, African American male who wore his football uniform and helmet on a cold November day as they stood on the football field as a cold fall wind blew by. The Strong Easy is a football play that the Chester Ridgely High School team had run for several years. It is an I-formation play where the full back stands behind the right side of the quarterback and includes a fake handoff to the fullback who runs toward the gap provided by the guard and tackle while the quarterback makes a quick decision to throw to his number one or number two receiver running a short curl route to the tight end on an outside slant route or the halfback running a wheel route. The play had been an effective play for Tyrone over the last two years while playing varsity football, based on his speed and ability to catch the ball.

"We have a couple of other plays to run," the coach said looking at his eager half back.

"Coach Edward, the game is tomorrow and it feels like you don't have me in the game plan at all. You know the playoff game is after this."

"Tyrone, I can't let you play tomorrow. Your grades are too low," the coach says.

Coach Edward Carter was a full time Baltimore City police officer and graduate of Chester Ridgely High School and enjoyed giving back to his alma mater.

Tyrone struggled with holding back his feeling of disappointment and his facial and body expressions showed his frustration.

"Are you serious? When I play, we win. You saw the scouts at the last game," he said defiantly.

"Where are you going to go if you don't get your grades up Ty? Get your grades up and you'll get the ball more."

Tyrone thought of an idea.

"Can I make a deal coach?"

"Go for it."

"If I make the honor roll, can I borrow your car for

prom?" he asked.

"What car?" the coach asked as he blew the whistle stopping the play on the field.

"That M6 you drive," Tyrone said pointing at the coach's royal blue BMW parked on the parking lot, visible from where they stood.

"Deal, but you have to play for my lacrosse team in the spring."

"Deal," Tyrone exclaimed feeling like he'd just won the deal.

November 19, 2016

Inside of the Ridgely Square Towers, a large fourteen story apartment building, Tyrone sat down at the round shaped wooden kitchen table reading over notes from class when he hears his mother, Sasha, enter their apartment. Excited that she was home, he stood and ran into the living room, finding her taking off the jacket that covered her blue scrubs.

Sasha, a beautiful slightly heavy set, brown skinned woman with short hair, smiled when she saw her son enter the room.

"Ma, I got a car for prom!" he happily exclaimed.

"What are you talking about?" she said in a raspy voice, kicking off her shoes and walking to her favorite recliner to sit down.

"Coach Eddy said I can use his car for prom if I make honor roll."

"Why aren't you at football practice now?" she

asked wondering why he was home this early in the day.

"My grades have been bad, but I'm getting them up. Look at the last two test grades I have from physics. I'll get them from the kitchen," he said and ran into the kitchen to retrieve them knowing they showed he received ninety and ninety-seven percent on the tests. He handed them to her smiling. "I'm also pulling up my grade in Algebra 2."

Sasha looked over the test papers.

"Ty, what are you doing? You know I can't afford for you to go to the prom," she said leaning back in the chair.

"Why?" he asked confused.

"I'm working under twenty hours a week now at the hospital. I have to do that in order to keep the Social Security Disability check that I get. If I go over the twenty hours, I lose the housing voucher and the check. My hours aren't guaranteed, so when I start working less than twenty hours again, I'll have to go back down to Social Security and argue with the case worker about why I need the disability money. I also may not get the voucher back which means I have to pay market rent with money I don't have. That's a risk we can't afford. I'm sorry, but I can't do it Ty."

"I can work. How about I get a job?" he asked.

Sasha turned and gave him a look of surprise that he would even suggest that.

"No," she answered thinking about losing her

housing voucher. Years ago, they were homeless and staying inside of vacant homes. After being linked to services specializing in homeless single parent families, she was able to get an apartment. Since then, she has been able to obtain a disability check for her diagnosis of Major Depression Disorder. Recently, she joined a work program that's given her part-time employment for minimum wage at Ridgely Square Hospital. While employed at the hospital, she took an interest in nursing and started going to college to pursue it as a career.

Fearful of the different factors that could cause her to lose the housing voucher, such as working over twenty hours a week, Sasha knew she needed to make Ty understand the situation.

"Let me try, mom," he pleaded.

"No. If you work along with me pulling any kind of income, the voucher will pay less in rent. That means you will have to pay for rent or I will have to pay at an adjusted rate."

"Well, how am I supposed to rent a tuxedo for the prom?" he asked frustrated with the situation.

"You're not going to be able to go. Bring your grades up, play football and lacrosse then get a scholarship. Don't put yourself in my situation and whatever you do, don't be like your father," she said, exposing a fear that she has always had that the street life would consume her son like it did his father.

December 8, 2016

Walking out of the library near the old Ridgely Market Place, and disappointed that his new girlfriend, Tina, stood him up, Tyrone placed two books into his backpack and noticed, Derrick, a heavyset dark brown skin guy with long dreadlocks, wearing a black Adidas sweat suit approaching him.

"What's Gucci?" Derrick asked.

Tyrone looked at his arm and noticed Derrick's Breitling watch.

"What's good Derrick!" he replied.

Derrick, a former classmate, reeks of marijuana smoke and cheap oil. The two walk together away from the abandoned outdoor strip mall area, that's plagued by vacant storefront buildings, homes, restaurants, litter, broken glass and discarded trash.

"Why haven't you been starting?" Derrick asked as he pulled a Black and Mild cigar out of his pocket. "You was breaking all them records and now you ain't playing. What, you hurt?"

"Naw. I got to get my grades up."

"If you ain't playing ball, you need to get your money up. It's disrespectful to be running around here with those dirty Air Max's," Derrick said pointing at Tyrone's dirty tennis shoes.

"My mom ain't got it right now," he said walking toward an alley filled with snow, turned over trash cans and clutter. Suddenly, Derrick pulled his arm.

"What if you could get it?" he asked showing

Tyrone a small revolver.

"I don't sell no drugs," he said looking around, annoyed by the smell of cigar smoke as Derrick puffed.

"No, but you will help me rob Jerry's Pizza and at this point, you have to do it," Derrick responded placing the gun in Tyrone's hand.

"Why?"

"You haven't played in three games. You know how much money I lost betting on your team because you didn't play? You going to help me rob Jerry's; I get money and you get money," Derrick said sizing him up.

"I don't want to do it."

Not wanting to get involved, Tyrone tried to hand back the gun.

"Put that away now," Derrick said in a forceful tone looking around to see if anyone else saw them. "You help me get this money or I'm going to kill you," he said sternly

Tyrone tried to dismiss the idea.

"I got homework," he mumbled shaking his head as Derrick pulled out another pistol.

"You think this is a game? I lost a lot of real money messing with you and your bum team. You going to help me get this money. Who cares about homework? You don't use any of that in real life. They ain't hiring niggas like us anyway. You want something, you take it. That's the American way. Ask the Indians," Derrick said as Tyrone placed the revolver in his pocket.

As the evening came, the sky darkened and the two walked together toward the carryout.

"Pull the hood over your head," Derrick ordered as they walk into Jerry's Pizza carryout.

"Alright," he replied, still not sure. He watched Derrick comfortably encounter the owner.

"Hello," Derrick said as the pot-bellied middle eastern owner walked out of the back wearing an apron and hairnet.

"Hello," the man replied and looked them over.

"Empty the register," Derrick demanded pushing Tyrone to the back as they walked up to the wooden counter that separated the register and kitchen area from the vestibule.

"What do you want me to do?" Tyrone asked.

"Take him to the back and get the money out the safe," Derrick said as Jerry, the owner looked on nervously.

"I don't have money in the safe," he said handing the money in the register to Tyrone. "Please take this and go."

"No," Derrick said pointing the gun closer to Jerry. "Get the money out the safe," he demanded.

"I don't have any money in the safe," Jerry said as Tyrone walked him toward the back.

"If he tries anything, shoot him," Derrick said as he noticed a police car pulling up in the front of the carryout. "No," Derrick screamed marching to the back and shooting Jerry in the back of the head. "He pushed the silent alarm," Derrick screamed as he ran to the back door. "Let's go!"

Watching his unlikely comrade run out of the door and being met by police, Tyrone ran back towards the front door.

"This can't be happening," he said to himself as two police officers pointed their weapons at him.

Officer Lake, a ten-year veteran of the Baltimore Police Department and Officer Moreland, a one-year veteran take in the scene as they waited for the offender before them to react.

"Freeze!" Officer Lake said. "Lay on the ground and place your hands behind your head!"

"Ok, you got me, I have a gun."

Tyrone placed his left hand in the air while attempting to show the police the revolver under the hoodie with his right hand.

"He's got a gun," Officer Moreland screamed as he and his partner shoot the offender several times and then panic as they watched his body fall lifeless to the ground.

December 9, 2016

The snow is lightly falling as a large group of protesters, residents, and media members are standing in front of the Southwestern District Police Station, as a result of the shooting the day before at

Jerry's Carryout. Minister Hakeem Andrews, a local preacher and leader for the Justice for All advocacy group walked toward a podium with the City of Baltimore's logo on it. To his left stood Ridgley Square's city councilman Bryant Dawson and the police chief, Alex Tillman. Many of the people gathered are protesting in anger over the recent video showing that Tyrone gave himself up to police prior to being shot.

"We want justice," Minister Hakeem decreed. "We have all seen the surveillance video of young Tyrone Clinton as he was attempting to surrender. He attempted to inform the arresting officers that he had a firearm and they shot him in cold blood. This young man, who had so much promise, has been snatched from us. We will not rest until justice has been brought toward the officers who killed this man." Looking around at the different news crews and the faces of the community, Minister Hakeem continued.

"Derrick Fulton was incarcerated and we commend the police department for their valiant efforts to restore order in the community and quickly respond to the call of a robbery. In that same light, we ask that the use of force policy be used equally. In no way, shape or form are we condemning the police department. We are calling for a progressive change to be made. We would like for the officers of this great city to live in this city and be a part of this community. We would like for the officers to be evaluated for any mental trauma or mental health disorders twice a year. We also ask that use of force documents be made public. If these fine men and women protect, serve and uphold laws to keep us safe, it is only fair that we feel safe from them and not have a severed relationship. If Officer's Lake and Moreland lived in the same city as Mr. Clinton instead of in their quiet suburban county homes, they might have taken a second thought before killing him."

He paused momentarily as several people clapped and others groaned. "They might not have killed Tyrone if he was a face they saw walking to school, to the library or from football practice every day. If they watched Tyrone's mother, Sasha, go to work at the hospital every day, they might have seen him as a human being instead of a perp, but we all know "maybe" doesn't bring this young man back. Maybe his death could save someone else's life."

The crowd murmured as Hakeem Andrews stepped away and the chief of police, Alex Timman began to speak.

"We completely understand the growing concerns regarding the use of force with our department. We also understand the strained relationship the community has with our department. While we are doing everything we can to mend that relationship, let's not forget what happened. Two young men entered the carry out with the intent to rob the owner with the use deadly weapons. The captured male,

Derrick Fulton shot and killed Mr. Jerry Abadejo, the owner of the carryout. Mr. Derrick Fulton ran out of the back door, surrendered and was taken into police custody. Close to the same time, Tyrone Clinton was engaged by our officers, Lake and Moreland. Mr. Clinton revealed that he possessed a gun which led to my officers feeling threatened after hearing a fatal gunshot moments earlier, which claimed the life of Mr. Abadejo. My officers acted out of self-defense and Tyrone Clinton lost his life. My officers have been placed on administrative leave while we investigate this incident. That is all we have regarding this case. Please be mindful that we still have an ongoing investigation with Mr. Fulton related to this and in connection to other open cases. Thank you."

Later that evening, Minister Hakeem Andrews met inside of the television studio for an interview. This was his fourth live broadcast interview since being recognized as a community activist, but this interview had garnered public attention due to it being related to an African American male being murdered by two white police officers.

"You are defending his actions?" Anna Cartwright screamed in her Nashville accent. She is popularly known for her years as a prosecutor and working several high-profile cases. After becoming Maryland State's Attorney, she was disgraced from office due to a scandal with the owner of the privatized prison company, Meyer Corporation. The scandal included

Anna Cartwright receiving financial kickbacks from Meyer Corporation from convictions, that included plea deals and stacked cases to increase the time on prison sentencing. She was now an investigative journalist who linked trends with convictions with judges. The names of the judges were removed from the publication. When the story made national headlines, she resigned from her position. Shortly afterward, she was given a nightly television show, broadcasting in Baltimore City, which allowed her to speak on current events.

"No one in their right mind would ever defend robbing a person at gunpoint," Minister Hakeem responded.

"I hear you, but you have been fighting for Mr. Clinton," Anna screamed back.

"Can I finish?" Minister Hakeem calmly interjected. "Mr. Clinton was wrong for robbing the carryout, but that did not have to cost him his life."

"He committed armed robbery!" she shouted.

"Ms. Cartwright, the surveillance video shows him surrendering to the police when he was gunned down."

"That thug was a danger to the arresting officers."

"Tell me, how was he a thug?" Minister Hakeem said angrily, knowing that Anna had a history of playing into stereotypes and giving misleading information. "Mr. Clinton was highly touted by several college recruits for his talent for playing football and his acumen for playing lacrosse."

"He robbed a pizza parlor," Anna screamed back, with the hope to lead the conversation into mocking the *Justice 4 All* movement. "His father, Paris Clinton, is currently serving triple life in prison. His mother lives in public housing and is a welfare recipient," she added.

"She works at a hospital and I didn't know that socioeconomic factors qualify you as being a thug," he countered.

The crowd listened to the exchange as Anna pushed back.

"His friend, Mr. Derrick Fulton, was put out of Chester Ridgely High School earlier in the school year. He was a known gang member and a bad person in general. This is who your victim chose to hang around, a person expelled from high school for bringing in marijuana and participating in an illegal gambling ring. Nancy Reagan had a campaign, *"Just Say No"* and your victim could have benefited from that campaign."

"It is public knowledge that Mr. Clinton did not associate with Mr. Fulton. Adding to that, you have made it a constant point to discuss Mr. Tyrone Clinton's socioeconomic surroundings. That being the case, you must agree with my recent campaign to reform the police department and stimulate cash flow in the inner city."

"How would you propose to stimulate cash flow in

the inner city?" she asked.

"By charging a tax to the people who work in Baltimore City that do not live there. That money would be designated to the inner-city schools and recreation programs. It is by far a better offer than what the people at Titan Industries have in play. They suggest that the homeowners in the Ridgley Square community, where this incident happened, sell their homes and property to them, so that Titan can build newer homes that the current residents cannot afford. They propose schools that will most likely be private that they can't afford to send their children to and stores they probably can't afford to shop in."

"How does your proposal improve the quality of life for business owners?" Anna questioned in a counter to his last statement.

"A person like Mr. Abadejo, who has had Jerry's Pizza in operation for over twenty years, has never lived in the city. He was a resident of one of the state's surrounding counties. He benefited from the people of that community, but his only return on investment was selling food. In theory, the tax I propose would make sure people, like Mr. Abadejo, have a vested interest in a place where they profit from if they don't live there."

"So, is that because of his murder in cold blood by these two, armed thugs?" she asked.

"No," Minister Hakeem quickly answered. "I am saying that if Mr. Abadejo, the arresting officers or anyone working in the city had a vested interest in the city, situations like this would decrease. There would be a larger sense of ownership and pride in the community."

"Why have you not made this a platform to run for office?" Anna asked realizing she will have to use Hakeem Andrews statements against him in order to create a deeper complex future story against the elected officials in Baltimore.

"We all know the election was earlier this year. My role is fighting for equality. *Justice 4 All* trusts and believes that the people in office, like the re-elected Councilman Dawson, will see the needs of the people and will continue efforts to improve the quality of life in Ridgely Square. I do believe that Councilman Dawson should take into account the people that voted him into office are being paid to leave by Titan with a community project he has supported. If the project with Titan Industries in Ridgely Square is completed, will the new residents that are targeted to be in a higher financial class, support him and his agenda?"

3

THE POINSETTIA CHAPEL

December 16, 2016

In a crowded large white colored chapel with red aprons next to the windows, two caskets are adjacent to each other. One with lots of toys, flowers and stuffed animals surrounding it and another with a large wreath with multiple roses in different colors.

"I'm so sorry," a male voice whispered with the sound of sobbing.

No one in the congregation appeared to have heard the whisper coming from near the coffin as a young female child's voice responded, "it's okay because we can spend time together now."

"You don't understand," the male voice whispered back.

The child's voice whispered, unheard by any of the bereaved. "Daddy, I love you. We never got the chance to spend time together because things got in the way. Nothing can get in the way of that now. I'm happy daddy. I love you."

February 8, 2016

Tiffany, walked into the kitchen of her apartment. At twenty-eight, she had seen and experienced a lot for someone her age.

"We are short on the rent again, Keyon." She was angry that they have not paid the cut off notice for the electric bill and the rent is three months behind. "What are we going to do?" she pleaded.

Keyon was listening, but not really paying attention as he drank orange juice out of an old McDonald's cup.

"I don't know, Tiffany. It's hard as hell to find a job. I'm trying all I can do." He spoke in a low tone to not wake up the children in the other room.

"Whatever," she said clearly upset.

"I've been trying to find a job, but I can't seem to find anything. Nobody out here trying to hire me with my record."

Keyon spoke without looking her in the eye so that she couldn't see that he was telling a half-truth. If he were being honest, he would say that he had searched for employment on some websites and local areas that informed him to complete an application online, something he never does. Oftentimes, he would search for employment with jobs that are looking for maintenance or construction work but did not return for the drug screening. With his background, he would be found out for sure.

At the age of seventeen, Keyon received his first

felony drug charge for the distribution of cocaine. He had an uncle, Herman, who he let talk him into taking the charge after the house they were in was raided. Though he had nothing to do with the sale of narcotics, he agreed because he and his mother lived in his uncle's house.

The courts mandated that he complete the Maryland Adolescent Addiction Program and after completing it, he returned home with his uncle and mother only to have the house raided again. During the second raid, the authorities found a large quantity of cocaine, marijuana and guns inside of the house. He once again agreed to take the charge to protect the family.

After his release from prison, Keyon tried to work construction and heating ventilation and air conditioning jobs with several companies that paid under the table. Refusing to go to prison again, he removed himself from his uncle and mother's presence by staying in a transitional home until he found his girlfriend, Tiffany, and eventually moved in.

"We have to do something different because we're using too much power in this place. We ain't got it like that and we need to stop acting like we do," she said cutting the light off in the kitchen and walking into the living room to cut off the television, her small attempt at using less energy.

"You're right. Maybe I could go out there on the strip for a little bit and sell something. I could get our money up until I can get a good job," he jokingly said following her into the living room. He was taken back when she turned with a serious look on her face.

"No! Are you stupid or dumb? That will just get you back in jail. Who going to raise these kids?" she bellowed with concerned that Keyon really considered selling drugs.

"What do you want me to do?" Keyon was trying not to argue because he loved Tiffany and they have a wonderful bond. He felt that he took on too large of a load in their household, raising children that are not his.

When he met Tiffany, she already had four children and now they have five once she had their daughter Kenya, his only child. With hopes to be more of a man than his father ever was, he made every effort to stay in his child's life, including being a father to Tiffany's other four children. The two oldest were ten-year-old, Darren and Desha whose father was murdered in prison six years ago. Tiffany never admitted to the name of the father of her eight-year-old daughter, Trinity. She created a backstory that she met the father at a club called Platinum, where they had a harmless one-night stand. After failing to have a successful match with other partners in paternity court, she realized that the man without the name was to blame. Several family members had speculated on who Trinity's father could really be but did not want to shame the family further. Her seven-year-old, RJ's father is currently incarcerated on two counts of murder. Kenya, four-years-old is Tiffany's youngest.

He loved Tiffany, even with all of the children and never looked down on her for having so many baby daddies.

"Go out there and find a job. I'm sick and tired of having to pull the burden around this house," Tiffany said as she scratched her head in wonderment. She didn't know what it would take to get him to take more responsibility.

"What do you think I do all day?" Keyon asked as Tiffany picked up the lamp revealing a sandwich bag filled with marijuana.

"Does this answer your question? You can't get a job if you not taking a piss test. You can't pass a piss test if your piss isn't clean. You think I'm stupid?" she asked in anger.

"It's just weed which is from the earth," Keyon tried to explain with humor, but failed. Tiffany wasn't moved.

"I have kids in here. Do you think they wouldn't find this? You know the state would have taken them from me if they had found this." she yelled.

"I'm sorry."

Keyon knew the last thing he wanted to do was cause any problems that could make her lose her kids, which of course included his own daughter.

"Yes, you are! Get out!" she screamed.

Keyon who was startled to hear what sounded like

her telling him to leave, looked at her questionably.

"What?"

"Get out of my apartment! I asked you to buy milk yesterday and you said you didn't have money, but you have money to buy weed? I don't need your help, get out!"

"I don't want to leave without my daughter," he exclaimed.

"Get out of my house Keyon. She's my daughter, too."

April 10, 2016

Florence Simms stood near the glass front door of New Hope Greater Love Church talking to her granddaughter, Tiffany on a Sunday morning, glad to be out of the hospital after a recent stroke. Having a difficult time maintaining her posture, she could remember how well she could stand in heels, similar to the ones Tiffany chose to wear to church today.

"Are you and the kids coming over today for dinner?" she asked.

"No ma'am." Tiffany replied, looking at Pastor Avery talking to a visitor while standing a few feet away on the concrete steps.

"Why not?" Florence asked as other members of the church left out of the church door. "You going home to Richard?"

Tiffany looked at her grandmother confused.

"What? I don't know who Richard is? I just don't

feel like dealing with your daughter today."

Tiffany wasn't quite sure, due to her grandmother's Alzheimer's, if she knew what she was saying or if she remembered the history with Linda and her husband. Though Daryl was the predator, she still had issues with Linda, her own mother.

"You have five kids, you know who Richard is. Plus, I miss the grandkids and I cooked your favorite," Florence said with a warm smile.

"Will Uncle Laurence and Tina be there?" she asked with a smile on her face. "I need to ask him some questions about college. Remember, my kids are your great-grands and I'm your grandchild."

"Yes, I cooked a nice, big dinner today. You know Laurence loves his greens and chicken. Speaking of which, I don't remember turning off the oven. You need to stop trying to confuse people with all these titles, grandchild and great grandchildren."

Tiffany smiled because she knew her grandmother was trying, but she definitely wasn't herself.

Will my mother's husband be there?" she asked, not using his name or the title daddy.

"You know Daryl won't show his face around this family because he's a coward. I do not understand why your mother is still with him."

"I don't want my kids around him," Tiffany said in a low voice, afraid of being heard by members leaving the church.

"Why don't you report him? It's never too late. It's

a shame your mother did nothing all these years."

"No ma'am, I don't want to see him."

"You know, I know what he did to you. You shouldn't have to go through that all by yourself."

"No, grandma," she blurted out in frustration. "I dealt with him for years and my momma protected him. I don't want to send him to jail and have to deal with more judgement and hate from her or anybody else in the family."

"What he did is illegal and he needs to be put in prison," Florence said angrily.

"It was also illegal to be a free black man and having the ability to read during the time of slavery. The legal system is a scam. I'm not happy about anything he did, but it is what it is."

"That's not the right mentality and he needs to be put in prison."

"Grandma, I want Trinity to have a normal life. The last thing I need is for people to give her a stigma over who her father is. How do you think that makes me feel being powerless to him all these years? I don't even want to speak about him out loud," Tiffany said feeling sick at the thought of her father and getting angry as his face appeared in her mind.

"Why don't you and the kids move in with me at the house?"

Tiffany huffed in frustration at the request. She loved her grandmother and loved that she wanted to fix things, but there was no fix for this.

"No grandma," she said.

Tiffany turned her head as she watched a car drive up the street extremely fast.

"Why?" Florence asked.

"I need to do somethings for myself. I had these kids and I need to raise them. You know you're nasty for that Richard joke."

"You know what's nasty is that thing right there talking to Pastor Avery," Florence said.

Tiffany turned to follow her grandmother's line of sight.

"Why?" Tiffany asked.

"That thing right there talking to your pastor is a man dressed like a woman."

"Really, grandma?" Tiffany asked, ready to walk off.

"Just because they try to force it on you, don't make it right."

"That person hasn't bothered you."

"And I ain't bothering it."

Tiffany shook her head in disgust.

"You just sat in church for three hours and you judging a person you don't know. Is that right?" she asked.

Florence chuckled and waved her off.

"Seeing that you are so saved, you're saying grace today," she joked.

May 16, 2016

One week after the first community meeting with Titan Industries, Tiffany stood to ask the company representatives to explain about the deal that had been made between them and the Ridgely Square Towers where she lived in an apartment.

"So, what are you saying?" she asked.

Back in less than a week for another meeting with the community, Chanel and Chandler Titan again sat at a table at the Senior Care Nursing Home addressing concerned residents.

"The Ridgely Square Towers has agreed to contract terms with Titan Industries. We do have plans to implode the apartment complex and, in its place, we plan to build a private community college," Chanel stated, glancing at Tiffany and her daughter Kenya before making eye contact with Pastor Avery and Florence Simms who were once again in the audience for the meeting.

"Where are we supposed to go when you do that?" Tiffany asked sternly with a panicked voice.

"We will provide all the tenants in your apartment complex with a ninety-day notice to move. Obviously, you won't be getting the seventy thousand dollars that several of the homeowners have the potential to gain." Chanel looked glumly at a few members of the audience who were shocked to hear her revelation. They were looking at her as if they didn't know this action was coming.

"Why is that?" Kenya asked. Tiffany looked down at her daughter wondering what she knew about money at her age. She was cute in her long, black pigtails with bright pink ribbons that matched her pink and white outfit.

Chandler was amused by the child's question considering how young she was. He smiled down at her and tried to answer in a way that she would understand.

"Well, when you rent you don't own. When you don't own, you don't have a stake in getting what a person who owns a house has. You can't get money out of a house that isn't yours."

He then turned his attention back to Tiffany.

"To be fair, ninety days is a lot of time to find a different place and we don't have to provide that, but we're good people."

Chanel took over the conversation.

"That being said, we have a signup sheet for affordable housing in Woodlawn if you can't afford market rent elsewhere." She placed some papers on the table in front of her signaling where renters could sign up.

Tiffany wasn't buying it and hearing she would have to move and uproot her children didn't sit well with her.

"My children are in school and that means they will have to transfer."

"To be honest, Ridgely Elementary, the school that

many of these kids are zoned to attend will be shut down by the end of this school year. Councilman Dawson, who approved this project and represents Ridgely Square, but is not here tonight, informed us that the school is one of many not in the budget for the next school year. At least your child has the opportunity for a fresh start in a better school. We didn't make the choice to sell your apartment building, your landlord, the apartment owner did." Chanel pointed to the sign-up sheet, again encouraging Tiffany to sign it.

Defiant 'til the end, Tiffany didn't move, but ignored the gesture and continued with her plight.

"So, because I don't own a home, I don't have a say in this?" she asked. She glanced in her grandmother's direction and watched as she looked down at the off-white tile floor probably thinking that the light is starting to give her problems concentrating on the voices. That has happened to her before and she knew the signs.

"The school is something you should definitely talk about with your Parent Teacher Association," Chanel interjected. "Are you involved with them?"

Tiffany could tell by the undertone of Chanel's words that she was trying to insult her as if to say not many African American parents were involved in their child's PTA.

"Does it matter?" she asked.

Chanel paused to see if she would get an answer

and not hearing any, she again pointed to the sign-up sheet.

"You can write or call your landlord if you have any other questions, we are here to speak directly with the homeowners and businesses owners in this district, but we didn't want any of the renters to feel left out."

Tiffany started to continue their back and forth, but she again looked over at her grandmother and was concerned with the expression on her face. Rather than continue, she chose not to respond to Chanel.

May 20, 2016

"Tiff, can I see my daughter?" Keyon asked, while in gray scrubs as he knocked on Tiffany's apartment door. The gray painted door and the sheetrock hallway walls created a small echo in the quieter than normal Ridgely Square Towers. He looked around but saw no one paying him any attention.

"Go away," Tiffany screamed back from the other side of the door.

He knocked again and this time the door opened and to his surprise, a guy, large and big in stature stood on the other side. He knew this was a guy that Tiffany had recently begun dating and he immediately went on the defense.

"Who are you?" he asked sizing him up, even though he knew who he was.

"Nigga, I'm daddy, who are you?" Tony countered.

"I'm Kenya's father," he said, trying to stay calm. "I

just got off work from the hospital and I'm trying to see my daughter."

"Hey, you got a job nigga?" Tony asked with a condescending tone, amusing himself and Tiffany. "What you do?"

Keyon looked from him to Tiffany and then back to him.

"I'm a housekeeper at the hospital. Look, I don't want any trouble. I just want to see my daughter."

"You don't have a daughter if you don't buy no books, don't buy no food and don't buy no clothes. As far as I'm concerned, I'm her father and you just some nigga with a title."

Keyon tried to hold his anger back, but the trite words from Tony got the best of him. Without thinking, he threw punches as Tony, who was much larger than him grabbed and threw him against the sheetrock wall creating a small indentation. He tried to comeback with a flurry of punches as Tony countered with a forceful overhand right hook causing him to fall. Fearful, he watched as Tony crouched on top of him and began punching him just as he sees his daughter coming toward them. He watched as a horrific look appeared on Kenya's face at seeing her daddy on the ground.

"Get off of my daddy!" she screamed.

Keyon didn't want her to witness what was happening and knew he'd made a mistake in throwing that first punch.

"Kenya, I'm sorry. Daddy is sorry," he said in a faint voice as the sound of police sirens are heard in the distance. Suddenly, Tony stood up and backed away. "I'm sorry," Keyon said again as he watched his daughter cry, but he knew not to make a move even to console her. He could hear the sound of police officers approaching as Tiffany pointed at him screaming in the background.

Willfully turning around and allowing himself to be handcuffed, Keyon saw the stream of tears falling down Kenya's face, causing himself to cry as well.

May 21, 2016

"Is he coming back?" Darrin asked as he sat in the bedroom with his sisters. With no air conditioning, the humid air flowed through the room providing no relief from the hot day. Around them, toys covered the floor, a bunk bed sat in the corner, a large flat screen television was mounted on the wall with a PlayStation 4 placed underneath.

"No, Darrin," Kenya said. "The police came and locked him up."

"I'm sorry about that," Desha said as she glanced at the dollhouse Keyon made for her for Christmas.

"I miss my daddy. Why did this have to happen," Kenya said picking up a doll to play with.

"I miss having him around, too," Darrin said picking up a half-built model car and showing it to Kenya. "Who's going to help me with my homework and finish building this? Your father used to help me build these and airplanes, too."

"He showed me the drones that he flew with you at the park," Trinity, their other sister said. "Is it our fault that the police came and locked him up?" she asked, watching them play.

"No, it's not," Desha said shaking her head. "He didn't come here to see us. He came here to see her," she said, pointing at Kenya.

"I wanted to see my dad, too," Kenya said sadly.

"Your daddy didn't care about us. He was only here for you. Now you're just like the rest of us," Desha said angrily."

"What does that mean?" Kenya asked.

"No father and poor." Out of anger, Desha slapped the doll out of Kenya's hand.

"I have a father," RJ, blurted out as he played with his race car.

"Being in jail is the same as being dead, idiot. He was the only person mommy has dated that liked us and Kenya ruined it," Desha said balling up her fists and walking out of the room.

"I didn't ruin anything," Kenya said in a low voice.

"You should have said something to mommy to stop the police from taking away Mr. Keyon." Darrin said thinking about how much he hated his mother's new boyfriend. "Mommy and Mr. Tony are out there watching television and eating and we're always in this room. Your dad never did this to us."

June 7, 2016

"I'm glad to see you outside of the jail," Pastor Avery said to Keyon as they sat in his office at the church.

"Thank you for coming to the jail to see me every week. It really meant a lot to me when you came and held chapel service."

"How long have you been out?" Pastor Avery asked placing a set of keys on the table.

"About four hours," he answered while looking questionably at the keys on the table in front of him.

"You have a place to stay or a job yet?"

"No sir."

"Good. I have a room upstairs that can serve as a little apartment and I need a groundskeeper here. The church can pay you, of course. You'll earn three hundred weekly and you don't have to pay rent. I just ask that you don't smoke, drink or fornicate inside of the church."

Keyon was excited. He felt like he was getting a break.

"Pastor, I won't disrespect the church. When can I start?"

"You already have. Your keys are right there on the table. I want to get a cheesesteak, so can you walk with me up the street to Jerry's? I'll get you one, too."

"I heard about the situation with Sister Tiffany and Brother Antonio. I want to make sure that a situation like that doesn't happen again, especially here," Pastor

Avery said as they walked.

"No, sir, nothing like that will ever happen again."

"Those kids like coming here and we love having them. Everyone has a story, brother Keyon. I know he wasn't right just like you know you weren't right. That being said, be a father to your daughter and let that foolishness go."

They attempt to cross the street as a car drives through a red light into oncoming traffic and continues driving inches away from causing a major collision. Pastor Avery pulled Keyon back before being hit by a car.

"People don't value life like they used to."

December 7, 2016

"How's your classes coming along?" Linda asked Tiffany as she glanced at Kenya watching her grandmother lying in a hospital bed. It had been close to a year since Linda had interacted with her daughter and grandchildren. Still confused as to why her mother chose Tiffany as power of attorney over her affairs, she tried not to show any sign of resentment toward her estranged daughter. She selfishly wished that she could say the words that would have her mother, daughter and her grandchildren at the house for Christmas in a few weeks. Realistically, her mother's health had taken a turn for the worse with the constant strokes, Alzheimer's and blood clots.

"They're coming along good, Ma. I should be done

with the nursing program next year," Tiffany said looking not at her mother, but instead focusing on her grandmother lying peacefully with her eyes closed. She wished she could have more chances to be with her mother like this, but she couldn't trust her judgement. The only reason she is talking to her now is because of her father's recent arrest for sexual assault, an event where she partially blamed her mother.

"You going to be doing this one day, huh?" Linda asked looking around the hospital room, still having a hard time thinking about the most recent stroke her mother suffered.

"Hopefully. How's daddy?" Tiffany asked as she looked at Kenya who was lightly touching her great-grandmother's hand as she lay still in bed.

"He still in jail. You happy?"

"Why didn't you do anything about it before?" she asked.

"Like what?" Linda asked.

"Like call the cops. When I told you what he was doing to me, you acted like it was a lie or a joke," she replied in anger.

"How was I supposed to know?"

"I told you. I didn't want anybody else to have to go through this."

"Looking back on everything, I was wrong. Is that why you stopped bringing the kids over?"

"I never wanted to start. I had to grow up with that

and none of them should have to experience what I went through."

Linda shook her head in agreement.

"You're right. I was five years old when my daddy left us. Momma and Uncle Daddy had to raise Laurence, Leon and me. She never got support from our father. She changed our names back to Simms and we never heard or spoke of our real daddy again and Uncle Daddy filled the father role. I know it ain't what a real family is like and I really wanted that for us. I wanted you to have a father and me to have a husband, but I'd like to point out that one of your kids has a father that's working and doing well for himself. Don't rob that child out of something good that you didn't have."

"What's that?" Tiffany asked glancing at Kenya and thinking about her other children.

"A father in her life that is trying the best he can. Your father is a piece of work, but he has always been a father."

Tiffany was not pleased at her mother's attempt to defend the actions of her husband. Without saying another word, she grabbed Kenya by the hand and walked out of the room in frustration.

December 8, 2016

"You sure I can take her?" Keyon asked Tiffany. He smiled as Kenya ran over to give him a hug. Feeling complete and whole by the embrace of his daughter, he closed his eyes and enjoyed the moment.

"She's your daughter, too."

"Of course," Keyon said opening his eyes and then the car door of his older model green Chrysler Neon, so that Kenya could get in. "I'm going to take her to the playground, to the movies and to grab something to eat. What time do you want her back?" he asked.

"She's your daughter. Take as much time as you want."

Tiffany turned to walk back to the apartment wishing her other kids had a father like Keyon. Thinking about the long day ahead of her at the hospital with her grandmother, she thought about asking Keyon to take the other children with him instead of leaving them with Tony, before noticing her Uber had arrived. She had let the thought of all of the children spending the day with Keyon go and got in the car for the ride to the hospital.

Keyon, happy to have Kenya with him, drove past the closed and boarded up New Hope Greater Love Church as he thought about providing his daughter the better things in life. Convinced that her greater life will start today, he looked forward to their time together at the playground as he heard the faint sound of dirt bikes with the engines revving up.

After sitting a few minutes at a red like, the light turned green just as one of the loud bikes being driven by a man with gray hoodie comes within inches of hitting his car. Swerving out of the way of the dirt bike and its driver, Keyon wasn't prepared when all of a sudden, he saw a black Mazda run the light and before he could react, the driver crashed into his driver's side door. The force of the collision drove his face into the steering wheel as the car with him and Kenya inside is slung into a street light pole. Holding on to a bit of consciousness, Keyon felt an unusual weight on his shoulder while turning his head just in time to see the driver of the Mazda running away from the accident. Having difficulty concentrating, smelling the scent of gasoline, he felt the warmth of blood running down his face just before noticing his daughter's left leg and arm draped over his shoulder. That's the last thing he remembered before losing consciousness.

4
THE PROTEA VIEWING ROOM

December 8, 2016

"I can't believe they have me dressed like this" a soft voice whispers over a mid-thirty-year-old laying inside of a coffin. The caramel skinned corpse is clean shaven with a short haircut, dressed in a dark brown suit, blue shirt and a brown tie.

"This is wrong, this is all wrong," the voice said.

Several middle aged and elderly people crammed inside of the small Protea viewing room as the song, *"I'll Fly Away"* is heard faintly in the background.

Sedrick and Erica Little walk toward the casket.

"You did this to me," a voice whispers. "I will never forgive you. You two never loved me, ever. These people are not here for me, they are your friends. You don't know anything about me. You never took the time to learn about me. After everything I've been through because of you two, you do this. I couldn't win with you in life and you spit in my face one more time in death."

"We would like to thank everyone for coming today. I know it was not easy for a lot of you to come up here on short notice, but I'm glad you did," Erica said.

September 9, 1988

"Second place again. Are you even trying?" a frustrated Erica said to her daughter, eight-year-old, Sabrina Little.

"Yes ma'am," Sabrina said in fear of her mother as she glanced at her twin brother, Simon, walking with their father across the busy street. Behind Sedrick and young Simon is a long hill, sports field and Ridgley Square Elementary School. Cars normally drive forty to fifty miles per hour on the four-lane road that separates the west and east bound traffic by a small concrete median.

Sedrick Little was born to Malcolm and Ida Little, the founders and owners of the international hotel, Grand Regal Suites. Erica was born to George and Brenda Scott who were the founders and principal owners of Psalms Airline. George Scott was a pastor and operated Psalms Airline as a Christian-based company. The Scott and Little families collectively thought it was a good idea to circulate wealth and arranged the union of Sedrick and Erica. Years after the death of George and Brenda, Erica mishandled the expansion of Psalms Airline, which soon led to her removal from the company's board. Sedrick continued to run the Grand Regal Suites, but grew interest in community development projects that Erica invested in. Using George Scott's "God First," principal of business, the two began transforming communities and made it a point to always present a religious image of family.

"What's the sense of me placing you in piano class if you can't succeed in any competitions?" Erica asked, irritated that her daughter failed in the latest Young Ladies of the Atlantic Talent Search competition.

Behind Erica and Sabrina are several large stone and brick single family homes and a three-story building with a sign that said Baltimore Metropolitan Social Club, a place she and her husband's families have been a part of for generations.

"I'm sorry. I will try to do better next time," Sabrina said, feeling bad that she had let her mother down.

"No, you won't. You're going to suck next time like you did the last few times. We just have lousy kids. How are you going to land a role as an actor without any talent?" she exclaimed pointedly. Dissatisfied at the efforts she'd made to bleach Sabrina's skin color, and straighten her hair, Erica pondered about what she would have to do to get her daughter to perform better.

"Why can't I play football or basketball? Simon wants to be an actor," Sabrina said looking at her father and brother as they waited for the traffic to stop.

"Simon is a boy and boys play sports, fix cars and lift heavy things, but girls sing, dance and act. We will find you a brand new piano teacher tomorrow," Erica scolded.

Sabrina was tired of the multiple extracurricular activities, like piano, ballet and theater.

"I don't want to do that, Simon does."

As Erica swatted her cheek, Sabrina glanced at Simon, who was standing across the street. She could see the look of disappointment on his face as he thought about his team's most recent loss. Looking at the ground and refusing to cry, Sabrina ran into traffic toward him as she is hit by a pickup truck.

November 10, 1997

Shooting a basketball and missing the rim, Simon is pushed down by a classmate charging towards the basketball while in gym class. Trying to pull himself up, another student on the bleachers yelled down at him,

"Get up queer," he heard.

The large gymnasium was a part of the William Bartholomew Preparatory School, located in Howard County, Maryland. The school has serviced many of the elite and affluent families in Maryland for over one hundred years.

"I am not gay!" he yelled defensively. He attempted to catch a pass and was elbowed by another classmate who intercepted the ball and ran up the court.

Everyone turned when they heard Ms. Franklin, the school's gym teacher, blow her whistle.

"Allen, get in the game and Simon take a breather."

Young Allen Bradley walked past Simon onto the court and turned to him.

"Are you okay?" he asked concerned for Simon. Allen felt sympathy for people not able to defend themselves.

"Yeah, I really wish we had a theater class," Simon said looking down and away from his classmates. He was unaware that his mother had been watching from a distance. He sat on the bleachers as the basketball game continued.

"Here, you just dropped this," Allen said handing Simon a silver chain and locket that contained a picture of Simon's deceased twin sister, Sabrina.

Recently, William Bartholomew Preparatory School began offering outreach scholarships to inner city African Americans and one of this year's recipients was Allen Bradley after he was dismissed from Baltimore City Public Schools for bringing a knife to class.

"Come here, Simon!" Erica shrieked while gaining attention from the other students and Ms. Franklin. Simon, ashamed that his mother created a scene in the gym, walked quietly toward her, placing the chain inside of his pocket. "I need you to act like a boy," she firmly said.

"Do we have to do this here?" he asked as some of the students look on, and others continue to play basketball.

"Yes, because I don't pay all this money for you to

come here and act like some gay weird person. It is unacceptable. I'm tired of you parading around the world acting like some freak," she intensely roared.

"Ma, this is who I am," he said as his voice cracked with fear of his mother.

Before he knew what was happening, she slapped him in the face.

"You are Simon Little, the son of Sedrick and Erica Little," she said sternly. "You are a representative of our family, what we stand for and the legacy that we have built. You don't get the opportunity to be like those other kinds of people. Stop embarrassing me and get back over there and play like a man!"

Giving a petrifying look at Simon and the students looking at her, she found comfort in their nervous reaction.

October 15, 2015

"You wanted to see me," Silk Diamond, a medium height transgender female said walking into the office, brushing her hand through her long weave.

"Yes," said Ms. Clair, with a stern face. She was the owner of Nubian Radio Broadcasting, the largest African American radio broadcasting company in the United States.

"Okay," Silk said looking around at the office décor and noticed several awards, platinum records, degrees and family pictures of Ms. Clair and her husband.

"Have a seat, Silk."

"Ms. Clair, is this about my slip up and saying the "S" word on air the other day? I sincerely apologize; it just slipped out. I know better than to curse on air."

"This is not about what slipped out. It's about what "S" you had slip in."

"What are you talking about?" Silk asked, leaning forward in the chair.

"Remember that man you were having sex with at the Broadcasters Uncensored fundraising event? The one that was knee deep inside of you, in the family bathroom?"

"Uh, yeah."

Silk couldn't help smiling, thinking about the man's firm hands and the smell of his cologne.

"That was my husband."

Silk sat stoically, completely shocked.

"I'm so sorry." That had been a wild day after that incident and then being embarrassed and escorted out of the convention center.

"Did you even know his name?" Clair asked as she placed a manila envelope on the table as Silk looked on in silence. "His name is Stephen," Claire said.

"Am I fired?" Silk asked.

"Yes. In this folder you will find your severance package. I will provide you with two months' salary along with a letter of recommendation."

"Where can I go?" Silk questioned raising her voice. Silk was now thinking about losing her dream job as her mind went back to a time when she was forced to quit the choir at her parent's church because of her mannerisms.

"You can go to Life 97.3."

"They already have a T-girl as a radio personality. There isn't room for two transgenders there. I always wanted to work here."

"Well, I always wanted to be married to a faithful husband," Clair said sarcastically. "At least you had your wish. I'm going to ask you to leave and take this envelope with you."

Clair leaned back in her chair before turning it so that she was looking away from Silk and out of the window at Baltimore City's Inner Harbor.

Realizing the conversation was over, Silk Diamond got up and walked slowly out of the office.

March 29, 2016

"I been out here for about two months. You sure I can get money like you?" Silk asked wearing a short cut denim skirt and cropped pink t-shirt.

"Yes," Gina, a middle aged, tall dark-skinned female with wide hips said standing uncomfortably in her five-inch heels. "Get your money up and get yourself another place. My name is Gina, but I go by Lady. There's no reason why a person that looks as good as you do have to stay homeless."

They stood on a corner near several vacant houses and three carryout stores. The area is commonly known as Ridgely North, an area that community associations and leaders of Ridgley Square separated themselves from due to the sex trafficking, drug activity and growing number of gay, lesbian and transgender renters. The Ridgely North area is also known as an art district that rivals another Baltimore community known as Station North.

"I'm out here because I don't have a job," Silk said as two cars pull up next to them.

"You're a woman and as long as you got something between your legs or on your face to please a man, you'll never be broke. These idiots will pay anything to get off without commitment," Gina said as she was about to get into one of the cars.

Looking at the face of the elderly male in the car waving at her, Silk reluctantly stepped inside of the car thinking of how much to charge and should she tell him that she was born a man. Before they drive off, he turned to her.

"Can you get it up for me?"

Amused by the thought, Silk nods yes, as the two drive off.

April 5, 2016

"I really need to shake this fever. I need my mommy because she would know what to do," Silk said to herself.

She was sweating profusely while sitting on the edge of an emergency room stretcher, turning on the television and flicking through several channels.

Thinking about the strict rules and the different social clubs she participated in growing up, Silk started to hate the thought of calling her parents. Remembering that her father's company forced them to relocate further south in order to maintain his position, she wondered how different life would have been if he didn't have that job. Thinking about her past, Silk sobbed as a doctor accompanied by a medical student walk into the room.

"Did you tell her," Dr. Soleit asked moving some of the falling brunette hair out of the way of her glasses as she glanced at the chart in her hands.

"No. I've never delivered this diagnosis to anyone before. I wanted to see how you would do it."

Passing for a white female majority of the time because of her skin color and light brown eyes, Ciara decided to let her hair grow natural. Since she has done so, she has noticed that the doctors at the hospital have treated her differently. Not sure if Dr. Soleit, who Ciara had been shadowing for the last four hours, thought she was the dumbest medical student in the world, she wasn't sounding too sure of herself.

The doctor turned her attention from Ciara to her patient.

"Ms. Diamond, do you have a history of substance abuse, like sharing needles?" Dr. Soleit questioned as she had an assumption of what the answers would be.

Tonight, was like any other night in the emergency room for Dr. Soleit, and this is not the first time she asked the exploratory questions to patients like Silk.

"No ma'am, I don't even smoke weed."

"Have you had any blood transfusions?" Dr. Soleit continued.

"No." Silk began to cry, fearing what the next question would be. Working several blood drives with the radio station in the past, she had become familiar with the line of questioning and the reason for it.

"Do you have a history of having sex with men?" Dr. Soleit asked.

Silk didn't verbally respond but shook her head.

"Are you saying yes, Ms. Diamond? I need you to give me a verbal answer."

"Yes, ma'am."

By now, Silk had begun have difficulty breathing and started to panic.

"Have you been having unprotected sex with these men?"

"Yes," Silk answered as the faces of the men she slept with ran through her mind. Feeling the breath escape her lungs and her heart beating louder as anxiety began to set in, she heard Dr. Soleit's voice as if it were an echo.

"I hate to inform you that you have tested positive for the Human Immunodeficiency Virus, commonly known as HIV."

"No, this can't be," Silk whispered, feeling that time had frozen as she began to cry and shake her head before laying across the stretcher.

"How many partners have you had in the last three months?" Dr. Soleit asked as Ciara herself became dazed and began to cry. Unable to listen further, she left the room as she began to lose control over her emotions after taking in Silk's overwhelming response to the diagnosis.

"I'm not sure because I lost my job last year and began prostituting to have money. I've been homeless for about four months."

"Our social worker might be able to get you into a shelter. She will also make some referrals for you to get some help with treatment. Your disease does not have to be a death sentence."

Hearing the words, Silk sobbed harder.

April 10, 2016

"Thanks for coming today. How did you enjoy yourself today?" Pastor Avery asked Silk as they stood on the stone steps in front the church.

"It was very nice. I haven't been to church in a long while because God hates me." Silk answered, but she still felt uneasy around the pastor.

"Why do you say that?" the pastor asked in a low voice so that other members could not hear their conversation.

"God hates all gay people. He hates gays, lesbians, vegetarians, transgenders, acrobatic midgets and on and on. You name it, it's on God's, 'you're going to hell' list. He probably has my name highlighted." Silk said rolling her eyes.

"If you feel that way, why did you come?" Pastor Avery asked in a concerned, yet sincere voice.

Silk hunched her shoulders. "I don't know. I'm all alone. I been staying at this shelter and I don't know how long I have to live. The one place that made me feel like I belong to something hates me because of how I dress or talk or what I'm attracted to. I just want to be loved. You ever felt alone in a room full of people, like nobody cares about you but they are all smiling at you? Like they have read the story of your whole life but never said hello to you once? That's me. I used to be an usher and choir director, but I got put off both departments because I acted too much like my sister."

Silk stopped short of revealing that her parents were once members of this church in the past. They left because they felt that his messages were not condemning enough of sin and consequences.

"Where is your sister now?" Pastor Avery asked wanting to hug Silk, but not sure if she would be open to a warm embrace.

Silk pointed at her own head.

"Right here. I like it here and I really wish I had honest money so that I could put more in the offering plate. Everything I touch or am part of is a curse. It's probably for the best I don't come back here no more."

"We don't care about your money. We do care about your soul. How you get your money is between you and God and none of my business. Are you looking for a job?"

"Yes."

"I have a member of the church, Brother Herbert, who is the manager at United Parcel Service. He's trying to hire someone right now. I'll let him know if you're interested."

"Thank you."

Walking down the church steps, Silk smiled for the first time in a long time.

April 15, 2016

"Are you sure you don't need a ride," the case manager, Robin asked. The lighting in the *Just Like Home* shelter brought out the freckles in her skin. The shelter is a large townhouse that sat on the border of Ridgley Square and Ridgley North communities.

"Yes, ma'am," Silk answered walking to the front door in a long black skirt and a white blouse. "My mother is going to take me. She came all the way from Florida to take me to this interview."

Unknown to Silk, her mother hired a private investigator to find her two months ago. After Silk left her family home at eighteen, they declared Simon as dead to anyone that searched for him. After learning that he had changed his identity to Silk Diamond and had been prostituting and homeless, Erica had hoped to use the homeless status as a method to talk Silk into being a normal man.

"I'm glad you two are back communicating again." As Robin walked back to her office, Silk walked outside to the street filled with parked cars, overflowing trash cans, broken glass from a car window and crushed cigarette butts, as a gray Acura RLX arrives.

"Hi, Ma," Silk said smiling as the window to the Acura rolled down. She was glad to see her mother for the first time since 1999 and excited to learn about the success of the family business. Silk attempted to open the passenger door and found it locked.

"What are you doing?" Erica asked in a loathsome tone. She was irritated after all these years that her surviving child still does not fit the image she and her husband had hoped for. She looked angrily at her child's presentation and was displeased. Rolling down the passenger side window halfway, she hoped that none of the residents in the area recognized her talking to a transgender.

"Getting in your car, right?" Silk answered. She was mystified when her mother rolled the passenger side window back up.

"No, you are not. I told you, you will not dress that way around me or around anyone I know. You are a boy and you will act like one. If you want to get this job, you will go inside and change your clothes."

Erica clamored, vexed at Silk's presentation.

"Mom, the interview is in a half hour. We are about twenty minutes away. Can we go please?" Silk begged.

"Not looking like some nasty freak. You will not continue to embarrass me this way." Thinking about driving away from the residential street, Erica looked at the time and thought about the meeting coming up between she, her husband and Chanel and Chandler Titan at Lawson's Steak House.

"Would you have said that to Sabrina?" Silk said, barely able to hold back the tears as she felt the mental pains from years of rejection by her mother.

"Your sister is dead. She is not coming back and you are a boy!" she declared.

"She lives in me, Ma. We are together as one. We are twins. We share the same soul. I can't control what she wants to do. If this is how she wants to dress, who am I to stop her? She is a part of me."

"You're not ready, Simon," Erica responded and drove away from the shelter, leaving Silk standing in the middle of the street sobbing with a broken heart.

August 21, 2016

"I have a friend named Omar and he said you can move into one of his rooms for rent for four hundred dollars a month. You make more than that in a night. Get yourself out of the shelter," Gina said watching cars drive by.

Gina and Silk continued to talk as they walked past a red light. Gina had visibly been losing a large amount of weight from health complications and a history of drug use.

"Yeah, I guess, I need a place to stay, so, I'll make it work."

As they walked, Silk noticed a familiar black Land Rover as it pulled over to the sidewalk.

"That's half your rent right there, so you better earn it," Gina said smiling while walking away from Silk. The neighborhood they were in was known for prostitution and drug activity where vacant homes and business provided cover from prying eyes. Some of the houses are boarded up while others have fire damage from previous gas leaks and accidents involving the homeless that have sought refuge in the abandoned homes.

Laughing back at Lady, Silk stepped into the car and looked at a regular customer named Cube. Born with the name Daryl Gibbons, Cube was molested by his uncle as a youngster. Growing up confused by the constant fondling, sexual acts and watching pornography with his uncle, Daryl internalized a lot of his feelings and conflicts of sexual identity. He received the nickname Cube by his cellmate, during his first incarceration for selling cocaine.

After marrying his wife Linda, he faced difficulties maintaining his extreme desires. Many times, the two would have conflicting ideas in their values on what passionate sex should be. Linda would grow sick at the thought of his immoral sexual proclivities because of her family values and religious beliefs. He found himself soliciting prostitutes for fulfillment.

"Silk," Cube said in a raspy voice as he pulled into an alley they frequented to conduct business. The alleyway had been a popular hotspot for prostitution and drug activity because of its secluded location in the Ridgley Square community, once known as the Ridgely Marketplace. After several of the buildings faced fire damage from the riots of 1968, as a result of the assassination of Dr. Martin Luther King, Jr., the area became abandoned. Prior to Titan Industries, no one made a bid to Baltimore City to rebuild and restore the area that once served as an outdoor mall with several stores, homes and restaurants.

"Hey, Cube. How you been?" Silk asked with a childish smile.

"I've been better. You burned me," he said pulling a gun out of the side of his seat and pointing it at Silk. Unknown to Silk, Cube suffered from Dissociative Identity Disorder and one of his many personalities had impulsive anger and violent behavior.

Silk tried to move away in fear, but was restrained by the locked car door.

"What are you talking about? Please put the gun down," she said in fear, having a gun drawn on her.

"You know what you gave me," Cube screamed, slapping Silk across the face with the barrel of the gun. "You out here spreading that virus to niggas. That's foul. That's super foul. I have a wife!" he yelled with fury and hate. Silk could even feel the wet sputum as it Cube sprayed it in her face every time he spoke a word.

"I'm sorry," Silk cried as blood began to flow from her nose.

"You are bleeding on my cream seats and you're spreading your AIDS everywhere."

"It's not AIDS, it's HIV," Silk screamed. Before she could get another word out, Cube pulled the trigger and shot her in the head, killing her instantly.

"Either way, it's the reason you're dead," he said.

Cube stepped out of the car, opened the trunk and retrieved a screwdriver. After looking around to ensure nobody was watching, he unscrewed the license plates, throwing them into the backseat. He thought about setting the car on fire and then changed his mind. Instead, he opened the passenger side door as the upper torso of Silk's body fell out. He grabbed her body and pulled it near a large dumpster overran with trash and debris. He placed some of the trash bags over Silk's body to cover it up. Since he decided not to set the car on fire, he called 911 to report that his car had been stolen. Hanging up, he walked out of the alley after retrieving the tags from the back seat of the car and leaving Silk dead amongst the trash.

December 2, 2016

Reading a newspaper clipping, the funeral home director, Allen Bradley, relaxed inside of his office as a couple entered.

"Mr. Bradley, I presume? I'm Erica Little and this is

my husband, Sedrick. Dressed in a dark gray St. John Collection suit, Erica extended her hand, giving an oddly firm handshake. The warm scent of cologne and perfume filled the office air as Allen placed the newspaper out of view of the Littles.

Erica and Sedrick sat down across from him, not pleased to have to make his acquaintance. No one wakes up happy about having to see a funeral director, especially not the two of them. With the busy lives they led, being in a funeral home wasn't on their list of things to do next in life, yet here they were. From where life had taken them, this was the last place they thought they would find themselves; a funeral home in Ridgely Square.

"I'm very sorry that we had to meet under these circumstances and I would like to offer my sincerest condolences. I've known Silk Diamond for a long time. I used to listen to her on the radio," Allen said feeling weird that the same people that he's had meetings with about destroying the community are inside his community funeral home.

"Simon. My son's name was Simon Little," Sedrick interjected with an unforeseen assertiveness.

"I do apologize. I went to high school with Silk and actually knew her before she started undergoing a sex change," Allen said, caught off guard by the family's demeanor.

"He," Sedrick corrected again. "My son was not a boy lover," he boldly proclaimed with a hostile tone and a fiery look in his eyes.

"I did not mean to offend you, Mr. Little," Allen pleaded, seeing the intense look on each of their faces. He had become familiar with the Littles since the last few community meetings with Titan Industries.

"We would like to have him cremated today and get everything over with," Erica said looking around the office and making little eye contact.

"Correct me if I'm wrong, but are you saying that you don't want a ceremony for your child?" Allen asked feeling uncomfortable with the conversation.

"No. We would like to have our son cremated and move forward with our lives. Can you please tell me what your fees are for cremation?" Sedrick asked with a deep thunderous tone, feeling the need to assert his dominance toward Allen. Sedrick recently began questioning how others viewed him as a father and a man since learning that his son had taken on the persona of a woman.

"We normally charge around two thousand for that and we add in the fee of the Chaplin, so it will bring the cost around twenty-six hundred dollars. If you want to have your child..."

"Son, Mr. Allen. We will give you four thousand if you burn my son to ashes and not disclose to the media his death or any of his service arrangements," Erica said correcting him.

Allen didn't know what to make of Erica's curtness.

"Well, your child..."

"Son," Sedrick Little said forcefully. He clenched his fist and became infuriated that Allen continued referring to his son as a woman. "I don't understand why you can't say son, or Simon?" he asked.

"Well, Mr. Little, your child had a legal name and sex change. Technically, and I do not mean any harm saying this, your child's name is Silk."

"My son's name is Simon Little," Sedrick snarled angrily. "I know the world painstakingly has a habit of accepting homosexuality and making everything weird. I really don't care what kind of embarrassment Simon attempted to make of himself parading around like something other than how he was born, but my last memories of him will not be of a freak. I named him Simon and my wife gave birth to a boy!" Sedrick shouted.

Allen surveyed the range of emotions on their faces and took a deep breath and attempted to make eye contact with them.

"Mr. and Mrs. Little, I apologize if I have struck a nerve with you. I understand that this is a very hard time for the two of you. Your child, as you would like to remember, Simon, was a very old friend of mine. He was also a very important person in this city. If I may, I would like to offer funeral services for you all, including cremation, for free, to provide a final send off for an old friend."

Allen smiled as they nodded in agreement.

"Very well. We would like a specific group to attend

the service that only includes our family and church members from here and Florida. We do not want Titan Industries or the media to be informed of the death of our son. I understand that he made a name for himself with the gimmick, Silk Diamond, but the public will not know of that vile character's death. On the program, I only want information about Simon Little placed in the obituary and nothing connecting my child to that Silk Diamond persona. If I so much as see a person that looks like they were involved in my son's foolishness, I will shut down this funeral home. Are we understood?" Erica declared.

"Yes, ma'am."

Allen decided to not push them and was already regretting his attempt to provide a final service for his friend.

"I have a suit at home that I would like my son cremated in and I will have it delivered here in the coming days," Sedrick said.

This time, Allen simply nodded without speaking.

5

THE CALLA CHAPEL

December 16, 2016

"Why are they all here?" a voice asks inside of one of the large chapels with wooden pew chairs. In the front of the designated viewing room is a large black closed casket draped with an American flag and several photos and flowers. "That's me," the voice says recognizing his face in a picture. "Ciara," the voice says sorrowfully while remembering his fiancé, Ciara, a medical student at Ridgely Square Hospital.

The Calla Chapel is one of the larger rooms inside of the Bradley Funeral Home, which is almost packed to capacity with police officers, members of the media, family members, current students and alumni of Ridgely High School. There were also several police officers sitting in the front of the chapel.

"Starks, Ritchie, Brown, Stone and Whittington," the voice utters with a fond feeling for his co-workers. The voice wonders where Captain Grimes is. Lost momentarily in thought, the voice of Edward Carter noticed his mother and family members walking into the chapel together as a choir sings the former coach and police officer's favorite song, *"It's a Highway to Heaven."*

May 8, 2016

"We need to really remember that we are servicing the community and these people live here. They should not be scared of us and we shouldn't be scared of them. We know the relationship between us and them has been hurt by the old guard, but it doesn't have to stay that way," Officer Edward Carter a veteran for thirteen years said standing up in the roll call room as other officers look on. Glancing at the desk in front of him with Captain Grimes, two lieutenants and a sergeant watching on, Edward turned to his side as he heard the groans of other officers.

"Sit down, nobody cares," Officer Murphy, an old bitter beat cop of twenty plus years blurted aloud, annoyed with Officer Carter's speech.

"Nobody cares? I live here while you live over state lines, so you don't have to pay city taxes. I participate in the community I serve. I grew up here. I went to school not too far from the area I patrol."

Edward was trying to make a point to his fellow officers. Besides being a full-time police officer, he also served as a part-time football coach at Chester Ridgely High School

"You, you, you. How many arrests have you made in the last fifteen days? How many people have beat your cases in the last two months? You're a waste of space to someone that wants to do your job," Officer Murphy said leaning back, reeking of cigarette smoke and beer.

"I don't come to work to lock people up. I come to work to make a difference in the community. When the jobs left, I chose the police force for a career. I didn't choose it to lock up the sons and daughters of the people I went to school with. I choose it to keep them and the people I went to school with safe. This job is not us against them. It's us making it safe for them. I wear this uniform as a privilege not because I want to be respected," Edward said, looking around the roll call room.

In the last eight months, the police department has been short staffed and many of the current officers have been overworked. Some of the police officers decided to not get paid for overtime, but use the extra hours as compensation time to have paid time off at a later date. The compensation time has created a list of new problems with officers because the paid time off positions had to be filled by officers drafted by other shifts for overtime. Captain Grimes had begun halting compensation time as of last week, to the displeasure of many colleagues with families and thriving personal lives.

"Are you talking now because of privilege or because you want to be respected? The way I see it, I lost respect for you after you started talking that roses and butterfly nonsense," Murphy said tapping on the desk with his pointer finger, annoying everyone in the room with the constant tapping sound.

"Officer Carter is actually correct. We should find ways to become more involved with the community, which is a part of our mission statement. We can continue this discussion tomorrow, so everyone have a safe shift," Captain Grimes said.

He took the time to also point to the mission statement printed in large letters on the wall behind him that read, *"To serve, protect and be an example to the community."*

May 16, 2016

"That is not the only way to improve this community," Officer Edward Carter said to the Little and Titan families as they sat in front of the panel. "Sure, this community has gone downhill, but strong arming the people here out of their community is not the answer."

"You are correct," Chanel responded as other community members listened. "We are giving them an option. There will be no school here in a few months, so where will the kids go? A better or a worse school? There are no jobs here, so what will people do to earn a living? There are no grocery stores that provide fresh food on this side of the city. Many of you have health complications as a result of the lack of healthy food. This is a fresh start for everyone."

"How?" Officer Carter asked, looking to Pastor Avery and Mother Simms. "Why can't the people here work and live in what you are developing?"

"Exactly," Ms. Johanna, a forty-year-old resident with a history of heart disease and trouble breathing which is related to her obesity. She has had a long history of attempted diets, but they always result in her purchasing fast food. "With all the plans you all have, Titan Industries does not have a plan to put a grocery store in this community? My doctor would be happy if I could buy fresh fruit, vegetables or anything unprocessed for once in my life."

"The world doesn't work like that. This area needs a fresh start," Chanel stated as others in the room chuckle at Ms. Johanna's statement.

"As a policeman, we thought you would appreciate the idea," Chandler said as a baby started to cry as the mother began having problems getting the bottled milk out of the baby bag. Relieved that the mother had the situation under control, he continued, turning his attention back to those listening. "Officer Carter we're offering less crime in this area and a positive scenery. Think about how the property value will increase, the job opportunities that will be available and the pride that will come back to this area."

"By driving out the people that live here?" Officer Carter inquired. "I want you to understand that we have community cookouts, block parties and crab feasts. Pastor Avery's church, before it was a church, used to be one of the only black owned theaters in Baltimore during the Civil Rights Era. You want to throw that away?" he asked.

"By a show of hands, how many people in here knew that New Hope Greater Love church was once the only black owned theater in Baltimore during the time of Jim Crow?" Chanel asked.

They looked on as no one raised their hand.

"This generation doesn't care about that. This generation doesn't care about the reason you're trying to save this community. Why keep things the way they are when we can change them? It doesn't make sense?" Chandler said wishing that the same group of people would stop opposing he and his sister.

"It can improve," Officer Carter said while also feeling defeated. He was disappointed he wasn't getting more support from the people who lived in the community. "If you have the money and resources to build all these great things, why not do it with the people who live here now?"

"Amen to that," a young woman blurted out. She too hated the idea of losing the house she inherited from her grandparents, but hated the distance she had to travel to feel safe, purchase food, clothing and items for her terminally ill brother.

"We're in the business to gain money, not lose money," Erica Little said looking in disgust at the woman who was speaking.

"Everyone in here walks out a winner if we build in this district," Chandler professed, concerned with Erica's facial expression. "Even you, Officer Carter, will be able to sleep at night. This district will be the best! Every cop will be fighting to walk this beat for eight hours."

"Our *Officer Next Door* program will provide police officers who work in Baltimore City discount housing. Just think about the opportunity to live in an oasis, right in the heart of the city," Chanel added.

"True, but in the process, you'll strip away the culture of what makes this city," Pastor Avery stood up shouting. "You come here with your ideas to make money, but you don't even know what makes the city. Baltimore has a culture, it has beauty, it has a soul."

"Baltimore is a death trap. Both of our twins died in this city," Erica said lying to the room about her son's death, that she and her husband had not been in contact with due to his sexual identity. In recent years she had told others that Simon was murdered by gang members in Baltimore City. "We did all we could to support our son after his sister died, but this city took our boy's life as well. As far as I'm concerned, this is the only option to save the city. Our son's legacy shouldn't be his death, but the changes we can offer the next child."

"By moving everyone out?" Mother Simms asked.

"People can move back in this community after the new development if they can meet the housing requirements," Chanel said.

"And, what are those?" Tiffany asked, angered that she would soon not have an apartment while feeling afraid for the safety and well-being of her children.

"They are having the income to pay a mortgage, a background check and the ability to pass an interview with our community board," Chandler said.

As the room gasped at Chandler's response. Chanel spoke up before anyone could ask another question.

"This is a planned community, not the same thing as what we have now. We're talking a premium shopping strip, restaurants, and private community college and that's just the beginning for everyone. The condominiums and townhomes will be breathtaking. Those that qualify for the seventy thousand dollars will have a great chance to move back here."

A younger male sitting in the middle of the room stood to ask a question of Erica.

"What was your son's name? You said you had twins. What was his name?" he asked.

"Simon. His name was Simon Little."

December 11, 2016

"I don't think she thinks you're an idiot. You're a medical student and she knows you don't know everything," Edward Carter said on the phone to his girlfriend, Ciara.

In the driver's seat of the patrol car, not trying to make obvious eye contact sat Officer Edward's long-time partner, Officer Stone.

"Ah, young love," forty-six-year old Officer Stone uttered looking at the screen on the computer in the squad car. Edward ignored him.

"I'll be home right after the shift ends. It's weird not having deacon training any more. I reservations for us at Lindenwoods," he said looking out of the window. Edward had started training to become a deacon at New Hope Greater Love Church in early January and watched the doors to the church close a couple months ago due to financial problems. The church, along with coaching football, had played a major part in his life and he openly expressed sorrow related to the closing of the church. He even changed his plans for proposing to Ciara due to the church falling behind with payments to Sage Realty.

"You didn't tell me about the game last night," the soft voiced Ciara questioned in excitement on the other end of the phone.

"Oh, I forgot to tell you that we won. I do wish Tyrone had been at the game, but we were able to rally around the fact that he wasn't there." Edward smiled at the thought of the star player, but he felt a hint of regret that his star running back had been shot and killed a day before the playoff game.

"He was there in spirit," Ciara said.

"I have to go," he said hanging up the phone. He looked over at his partner and showed him a jewelry box with a ring inside.

"Wow," Stone said.

"I'm going to pop the question tonight."

"Why would you do something that dumb Carter?"

Stone joked. "Take it from someone who has been in two failed marriages, it's the best choice you have ever made. She's a great girl. How many people luck up with a doctor."

"She's in medical school, but thanks."

"I love the speeches you continue to make in roll call every week."

"Thanks, for saying that. It's always from the heart. If only everyone felt the same."

"Some of these people power trip and you know that. Murphy, Banks, and Graves have been here since Norton was the chief. They got away with murder under him, Hogan and Hunter. Now that this whole situation is happening with the Clinton kid, everyone is trying to be political. I think you're the only person on day shift that actually lives in the city. That's probably why the citizens respect you."

"Yeah, I find myself thinking if I make enough of a difference or not." Carter looked down at his phone at a picture of Tyrone Clinton.

"I've never seen anyone do as much as you do in this city. You're in the church, you're in the schools, you live here and you're from here. If you ran for public office, you would win just because of your resume right there." Stone tried to lighten the mood by nudging him, knowing that Carter had been trying to hide the grief over the football player who was murdered.

"I like what I'm doing now. Did you see that?"

Carter said placing the phone inside of his pocket as he observed a teenager spray painting the side of a building.

Reacting, Stone turned on the patrol car lights and siren as they watched the kid drop the spray can and run toward the Ridgely North community.

"Stop," Carter yelled, getting out of the vehicle as the teenage boy froze in place and turned around. "Kennard?" Carter uttered in surprise as the boy reached into his pocket and is shot in the shoulder by Stone. Recognizing Kennard as one of the students that played on last year's lacrosse team, Carter approached quickly.

"He's got a gun, drop your weapon, let me see your hands," Stone screamed, panicking with a smoking duty weapon.

"Wait, Kennard what are you doing?" Carter asked walking closer to him, concerned about the gunshot wound.

"You're just like the rest of them and we thought you were different, but you're just like the rest of them," Kennard said, revealing that he was reaching for a pink piece of paper, not a weapon. Trying his best to hold back the tears from the pain, he dropped the paper on the ground next to him as the blood continued to flow.

"What's that?" Stone asked as Carter called for an ambulance.

"It's a report card! You shot me over a report card,"

Kennard yelled while looking around in pain before laying back.

"You were going to show me your report card?" Carter asked.

"No, I was going to show you Ty's report card, Coach. He made honor roll. The grades came out on Friday. He really wanted to drive your car for prom. I think he cared more about that, than he did about playing football," Kennard said before closing his eyes.

~~

As the sky began to darken, the media reported the latest shooting of an unarmed African American teen, this time for having the report card of the recently murdered robbery suspect, Tyrone Clinton.

The growing number of protesters and members of the media stand in front of the University of Maryland Medical Center, where Kennard was transported by ambulance. Walking through the lobby, Edward is met by Captain Grimes.

"You need to go home. The tension has been pretty high between the protesters and police since the Clinton boy was killed. This just made things worse," he exclaimed.

"Cap, I know that kid and he's a good kid. I think it would be good for his parents to hear from me what happened," Edward said.

"I don't care if he's one of the kids you coached, I'm giving you a direct order to leave," Captain Grimes demanded as shouts outside of the lobby grew louder.

"Cap, a lot of these people will respect what I have to say more than any other officer."

"We can't keep them out of here. Some of these people are visiting loved ones. You have to go and leave through the ambulance bay."

"Have you spoken to his mother?" Edward asked.

"Leave now," the captain ordered as two young people dressed in black stormed through the lobby opening fire on the police officers standing guard. As gunfire is exchanged, Captain Grimes glanced over to find Edward slumped over a receptionist's counter near the front door.

"Ed," he said touching his shoulder. "Eddy," he said louder and in a more forceful tone. Feeling his neck, he tried to find a pulse. Not able to find one, he called a signal thirteen on his walkie-talkie, a code Baltimore City Police Officers used when they are in distress or in the middle of a conflict.

December 12, 2016

On a cold and windy morning in front of the Southwestern District Police Station, the chief of police, Alex Timman looked on from behind a podium at a small crowd of citizens, members of the police station, retired and currently serving police officers.

"Yesterday, as many have heard from the briefing, an unarmed African American male, Mr. Kannard Lyles, was shot by one of the responding officers for vandalizing a building in the Ridgely Square community. The responding officer, whose name is being withheld due to an investigation, reported that the suspect reached into his pocket and my officer was not sure if the suspect was trying to pull a weapon on him or not. After the incident took place, Mr. Lyles was transported to University of Maryland Medical Center. After we held the briefing yesterday, several protesters went to the hospital as well and some protesters took it upon themselves to open fire at several of my officers in the lobby, not taking into regard their safety, the staff at the hospital or other visitors. During the exchange of gunfire, two of the attackers were subdued. One of our officers was found pronounced dead on the scene as a result of the gun fire."

Feeling angry that the number of supporters for the fallen officer is very low in comparison to Tyrone Clinton that actually committed a crime, Chief Timman paused. Hearing several reporters ask questions about Kannard Lyles, but none asking about Officer Carter, Timmon continued.

"Officer Edward Carter will be missed. He was invested in the Ridgely Square community, a graduate of Chester Ridgely High School, deacon in the church and a football coach and he lived in this community. He wore his badge with pride and honor and was up for a promotion soon. He was a great man." The chief paused and looked out over the crowd, angered by the lack of respect for Officer Carter. Ignoring the uncomfortable glances, he continued.

"Some of you may be asking why I'm sharing this information and I might face reprimand from our mayor for doing so, but we are people, too. We might not do everything right, but Officer Carter was the standard of what a police officer in this city should be. He does not get the *Justice 4 All* treatment, which I don't understand why because, he was an African American. He did everything he could to help African Americans in this community not get locked up. It seems like when something doesn't fit the narrative, it's not news. I'm sure many of the media members wanted to ask about Kannard Lyles, which I have heard questions while I was talking. Let us remember, this is a stressful job and the safety of my officers is just as important as the safety of the citizens. When my officer shot the young man, I understood that he was fearful of what the suspect was retrieving from his pocket. There was no malice or ill intent. The people that shot at my officers inside of the hospital had vindictiveness and ill intent. Not one *Justice 4 All* member condemned those young people for killing one of my officers. Not one has reached out to Officer Carter's family, but they want to question our practice. The officer that probably would have agreed with them, was killed by them."

"Has anyone talked to the parents of Kannard Lyles?" a reporter asked loudly through the gust of wind.

"Did you hear anything I said?" Chief Timman yelled before slapping the podium and walking away from the small crowd. Feeling that today might have been his last day in the position due to his actions, he was content with what he said publicly.

6
THE MONTE CASSINO CHAPEL

December 16, 2016

"Why did my life have to suck God," a whispering voice said over a closed pink colored plastic casket. "Like seriously God, why me?"

A frail woman, in her late forties walked into the small viewing room and sat in the third row adjacent to a fireplace.

"I don't know who you are," the soft voice of Tina said as the woman began to cry. "I don't need your pity and I don't want it either," Tina whispered as the woman continued to sob.

"Just my luck, they had my funeral here and not at my church. I bet they didn't even tell Pastor Avery that I'm dead. Am I going to hell, God? My whole life has been hell. Are we capping it off with the same old routine for me?"

March 9, 2009

"Serena Williams has so many grand slam titles and Venus Williams has won gold medals in the Olympics," ten-year-old Tina declared to a classroom full of students patiently waiting for their teacher, Mrs. Matthews to come back. She had gone to the faculty area to print copies of the day's assignment.

"Why do you always talk about them?" one of the students said, annoyed and tired of Tina's enthusiasm over the Williams sisters.

"Why aren't you talking about them? Do you have any idea how many grand slams they have won all together?" Tina asked.

"Thirty. Did she win thirty or sixty, Tina?" another student asked as the class laughed.

"Stop making fun of her," ten-year-old Tyrone Carter said in her defense as the other students continued laughing and throwing balled up balls of paper at her.

"It's not funny. Do you know how intelligent you have to be to play tennis?" Tina asked, pouting.

"Do we care?" another student in the class asked, drawing a picture on his desk.

"You should because tennis is like playing chess. There is a lot of movement and planning that goes into tennis. It's not like running and hitting the ball. It's a lot of strategy and planning. It's like chess. Have you seen them speak on the Black List?"

"What's that?" Tyrone asked as the class began to quiet down.

"It was an HBO special that talked about different black people's rise to success," Tina answered.

"Then why do we care? Do you even know how to

play chess?" a male student asked as Tyrone threw a balled-up piece of paper at his head.

"No, but I want to learn," Tina replied feeling embarrassed.

"Do you know how to play tennis? I always wanted to learn," Tyrone said.

"No. I wish they had it at the recreation center," Tina answered in a low tone.

Hearing a noise at the classroom door, all of the students faced forward and looked at the chalkboard as the door opened, in fear that it was Mrs. Matthews entering the room.

June 2, 2016

"Sit down," Florence Simms demanded in a light voice as seventeen-year-old Tina looked concerned while pulling the chair out from the old wooden table. Sitting down while looking at the magnets and pictures on the refrigerator, she is handed a glass cup filled with her grandmother's sweet ice tea by her aunt Linda.

"I need you to listen to me good, okay? I don't have all the details yet, so don't get upset with me, we clear?" Florence said while sitting at the end of the table, preparing herself to be the bearer of bad news.

"Yes, ma'am." Tina answered nervously.

"Your father was robbed and shot today. They said he died on the way to the hospital."

Florence felt the best way to break the news was to

blurt it out. After saying the last word, Tina began breathing hard and teared up. Florence paused as her own tears fell down her face thinking about the death of her son, Laurence. Glancing at the refrigerator, she saw a picture of her and her children at a family reunion at the state park. She remembered Laurence's loud laugh and how great he was with kids. "I can't believe this is happening," she said.

"Where am I supposed to go?" Tina asked. "Daddy was going to take me shopping today? Grandma, what am I going to do?" she cried.

"You can stay with Daryl and me. We can't find your mother to tell her the news about Laurence, but you can stay with us until everything gets sorted out," Linda said placing her arm over Tina's shoulder to comfort her.

"I don't have a mother," Tina cried. Knowing that her mother, Gina, had chosen her drug habit over being a parent, Tina pretended that she never had a mother. She told people that her mother died while giving birth to her or that she was in the military, stationed in a foreign country.

Her earliest memory of her mother was of a group of men physically assaulting her father and stealing items out of the house to pay a debt. Her last memory of her mother was having her five-gallon water bottle, which was used as a piggy bank, emptied and her Disney movies taken to a pawn shop. She recalled the argument her parents had on the top step in front of the house as a result of the stolen money and movies. Knowing that her dad had the five-gallon bottle almost filled to the top with change and her mother emptied it just to get high, Tina heard whispers from her grandmother and Aunt Linda that Gina was seen in South Baltimore getting high.

"I'll stay with you Aunt Linda," Tina said wishing that her grandmother was an option. Knowing that she had been facing difficulties walking and remembering things, along with her series of strokes, she knew it was best to stay with her favorite aunt.

August 25, 2016

"How was school today?" Daryl "Cube" Gibbons asked Tina as he laid on the couch next to the front door with his shirt off watching a court show on television. His mood has been strange for the last few days, watching television nonstop and never going to sleep and talking more than usual. Her aunt Linda ignored the behavior because she was not sure if it was another one of her husband's personalities or manic reaction due to his stolen car.

"Hi, Uncle Daryl. I have to do my homework. Can I use the kitchen table? I didn't know you were off work today," Tina said, feeling that it was odd that Daryl had his shirt off in the living room.

"Some kid stole my car on Sunday. I couldn't get a ride to work. No worries. You can sit right here," he said patting the couch with a childish like demeanor.

"You can turn the light on if you like. Your aunt went to the hospital to check on your grandmother. She hasn't been doing too well and I think she had another stroke or something. Don't let me stop you though. Turn on the light and do your homework," he said.

"It's a little too dark in here, plus you're watching television," she said noticing that the white plastic blinds and burgundy curtains are closed.

"There's nothing wrong with background noise. It's almost prom season ain't it?" he asked, standing up and looking at her as several thoughts run through his mind.

"No sir, school just started," Tina answered backing up, noticing his eyes rapidly moving left-to-right.

"Anybody ask you to the prom yet?" he asked walking toward her and blocking the entrance to the kitchen. Looking at her, Daryl thinks of how she would look with her prom dress on. His voice deepened as his muscles began to flex.

"No, sir," she replied, confused by his mannerisms and somewhat fearful.

"Somebody should have taken a liken to you by now. It's a shame them kids at school would let all of this go to waste," he said looking up and down Tina's young body as uncontrolled impulses take over. He placed his right hand on her shoulder, not realizing how wrong his actions were.

Feeling uncomfortable, Tina attempted to move as he clamped down with his grip and wrapped his left arm around her waist, pulling her closer to his chest.

Tina didn't know what was happening, but she knew it was wrong as fear like she'd never felt before overcame her.

"Please, stop," she said in a soft voice trying to get away, but still being respectful of her uncle.

Daryl snarled.

"You come in this house looking like a grown woman today and I'm going to make you into a grown woman," he said grabbing her behind and moving himself closer to her.

"Uncle Cube, please stop. Please Uncle Daryl, stop! Please!" Tina screamed and panicked as he forced her to the couch, while forcefully snatching her clothes from her body. Tina was helpless.

~~

The front door opened and Linda walked into the house, unsure of the scene before her. Shaking her head as if to clear her vision, first shock and then anger surfaced as her gaze landed on her niece who was trying to redress herself with torn and disheveled clothing.

"What are you doing to my husband?" she screamed at Tina.

"Help me, Aunt Linda," Tina cries while also trying to grab the remainder of her discarded clothes from the floor to cover her naked body. Daryl, still out of his mind, tightened his grip, on Tina trying to pull her back to the sofa where he still laid naked. He still hadn't realized Linda had entered the house and was now standing before him taking in the scene.

Looking at Tina trying to push away from Daryl, Linda thought about the stories her own daughter, Tiffany had told her about Daryl. Visions of the daughter Tiffany had that she knew was Daryl's caused her to see fire as she became enraged with murderous thoughts. Going into action, she snatched a large family picture off of the wall and hit Daryl on the side of his head with it, causing him to fall away from Tina as the glass from the frame exploded on the carpet. As memories of Tiffany crying to her about her husband's previous inappropriate behavior flooded her mind, Linda knew she had made a mistake defending Daryl for years. Stunned by what she sees, she didn't know what to do next. She was torn between her loyalty to her niece and her loyalty for her husband. She didn't know if Daryl or Tina was at fault.

"What are we supposed to do with her?" she said through clenched teeth.

"You hit me," Daryl screamed. Blinking his eyes rapidly he smirked then turned toward Tina who was still trying to get away. He grabbed her left leg just as Linda hits him again, this time in the back of the head with greater force than the first strike and this time, knocking him unconscious.

"Look at what you made me do. Don't call the cops, they're going to arrest him," Linda demanded as she paced back and forward as Tina attempted to stand and move away. Linda's mind raced with ways to explain that Daryl did not have control of his behavior. Images of Tiffany crying with bruises on her face and arm flashed through her mind. Knowing that Tiffany had warned her about Daryl in the past, she felt that her big, happy family was ruined because of Tina. Linda did what she has always done as she leaned down to Daryl on the floor to console him and not her niece, as he lay unconscious on the floor. She can faintly hear the sound of her niece's plea.

"Help me," Tina cried again finally gaining Linda's attention.

Scared that her family would further alienate her, Linda grabbed her phone and reluctantly called 911.

~~

"I haven't seen you since the church closed," Ciara said looking at Tina as she sat on an examination table in the hospital. Ciara nodded to Officers Lake and Moreland, who escorted Tina to the Ridgely Square Hospital, letting them know that everything was okay as they turned to leave. Ciara felt uncomfortable learning of the sexual assault because she attended church with Tina and the Simms family.

"My life has been hell lately," Tina said trying to avoid eye contact with Ciara. The two have known each other for three years while they attended the New Hope Greater Love Church.

"I'm sorry about what happened to your father. He

was a good man," Ciara said looking at Tina's chart.

"Thanks. Why are you stalling. I know you have something to tell me," Tina said thinking about what her father would have done to her uncle if he were alive.

"There's no easy way to tell you this. We did the full test on you and it seems that you contracted gonorrhea and HIV from the man that raped you. I have a social worker named Trish on her way in to talk to you about options."

"Options? Am I pregnant" Tina asked wondering how could today get any worse.

"No, we did test for that and it came back negative, thank God, but we do have options for treatment and housing. Trish is really good at helping in these situations."

Trying to avoid eye contact because she actually knew Tina and felt sorry for her, Ciara looked down to hide what she knew was a look of pity on her face, though she wished she could be more compassionate.

"Thank God? You just told me, I have gonorrhea and HIV and you said thank God. Why should I thank God? Because I'm cursed? I'm marked for life and you want to thank God? Where and why am I thanking God? Because I'm not pregnant? So, I don't have to pass it on to another child? Is that it? Well, thank God that my child's uncle is not also his daddy!" Tina said agitated at Ciara's choice of words.

"Tina, I really didn't mean any harm. We do have

medication that can cure the gonorrhea and as for the HIV, we have treatment options for you that will allow you to live a normal life with it as long as you take your medication."

"Leave me alone, Sister Ciara," Tina said, lowering her head in shame and not wanting to disrespect a person she had a lot of respect for.

They both looked up when a woman walked into the room.

"Hi, I'm Trish. I'm going to be your medical case worker."

"I don't care," Tina said sullenly while looking at Trish's blue Miu Miu shoes.

"I understand that this can be a hard time to comprehend everything going on," Trish said looking at Ciara questionably. Trish had spoken to Ciara earlier about Tina and she was under the impression that Ciara and Tina had a history outside of the hospital. Figuring that the previous dynamic between the two would have made this atmosphere easier to manage, Trish was taken back by the dark cloud that loomed in the room over Ciara and Tina.

"Do you tell every rape victim this script?" Tina murmured thinking about the times she and her father went to the playground and to the US Open to watch the Williams sisters play tennis. She thought of the times they had won awards after facing tough challenges. "Please don't answer that because it was rude of me," she added.

"It's okay," Trish said pulling a chair up next to Tina's knees and sitting down trying to make eye contact. Realizing that her own demeanor may come off as cold, Trish thought of a different way to approach Tina.

Trish served on-call at the hospital to pick up extra money to pay off her credit card debt. Her bad spending habits and frequent vacations led to her growing debt problem. She applied for the on-call position four months after being appointed director at her full-time job at Greater Baltimore Substance Abuse Treatment Center. The hours at the hospital and deadlines at the treatment center have weighed down on her, making her a less than pleasant person to be around. She attempted to show a false face of control and empathy, but it was viewed as arrogance and agitation.

"Here are the facts. This is not a good situation. I would love to have met you outside of here in a different situation, but I didn't. I'm sorry that your uncle did this to you and he is in police custody right now. None of this is your fault and not one thing that happened is something you did wrong."

"Then why am I cursed?" Tina asked thinking about her father's death and her grandmother's failing health.

Trish searched for the right words to say.

"This is not a blessing, but I don't think you're cursed. Ciara told me about your loving family and how great you're doing in school. I know this is not easy, but do you have any other family or friends you can live with?"

"My grandmother," Tina responded wondering why Trish had asked that question.

"I'm afraid you cannot stay with her. She's suffering from several health complications related to her Alzheimer's and may be too much of a risk for you. Do you have an aunt or uncle you can live with?"

"What's wrong with my Aunt Linda now that my uncle isn't there anymore?"

"No, we are removing you from that home. We do not know how long your uncle will be held, so to keep you safe, we can't allow you to return to that house. What about your mother?" Trish asked.

"I don't have a mother. She died in a war," she lied.

"Oh, what war did she die in?" Trish asked.

"The war on drugs. She was on the front lines taking all the shots," she said looking away from Trish and at Ciara with a callous expression of rage.

Feeling the anger in Tina's tone Trish stood up.

"I understand that you are upset. I am ending this session a little early. I would like for you to know that if you cannot pick a place to live soon, we might have to place you in foster care. I'm trying not to do that because you could age out of care there and at your age, I can't guarantee a successful match."

"What about my pastor," Tina asked sarcastically.

"He's a widow," Ciara answered in a low tone to

Trish. "His wife died a few years ago. He's a really great guy and he has a great relationship with the Simms family. I haven't spoken to him in a while but..."

"I'm sorry," Trish interjected. "He's a widow and that's a risk I won't take after this child was just raped by a man who was left unattended with her."

"Well, if I age out of foster care, can I just move back into my daddy's house?" Tina asked Trish before she closed the door behind her. Feeling that Trish didn't hear her, Tina looked at Ciara as she updated the chart.

"You don't know, do you?" Ciara responded feeling empathy. "Your Aunt Linda sold his house to Titan Industries to help cover your grandmother's hospital bills."

October 20, 2016

On a cool fall day, slightly past four in the afternoon, Tina, wearing a jean jacket over a blue-V-neck shirt and denim jeans, accented with a Breitling watch that had once belonged to her father, stood alone over her father's grave in the Amber Walking Cemetery, a place that was left unkempt by the groundskeepers. She looked down at his headstone while hearing the faint sounds of cars driving by the residential street just behind her.

She was undeterred by the shoddiness of a cemetery that had a history of open graves and human remains scattered about, along with unmanaged grass, weeds, a burned down tool shed from a thunderstorm and stray cats. Oftentimes, prostitutes and drug users used the cemetery to do their business due to the lack of visitors of those who were entombed in the ground at their final resting place.

Decades have passed since Amber Walking was a high-quality cemetery. It had been well-known as the final resting place for many former slaves and civil rights leaders, among them being Chester Ridgely, an escaped slave from the Johns Hopkins plantation who frequently went to Virginia to escort slaves to freedom in Pennsylvania. After organizing a successful rebellion in Southern Maryland at the age of sixty, he went into hiding in the community now known as Ridgely Square until his death from diabetes.

"Why did you leave me, daddy?" Tina cried. She opened a letter that she had written earlier in the day to read aloud to him. "Hi daddy, it's me again, Tina. I miss you and I don't know where the future is taking me. I can't see myself in the mirror anymore. I see flashes of you, grandma, Aunt Linda, Tiffany, Kenya and Desha. I don't know what the flashes mean. I'm drowning and no one is here to save me. I hate you for leaving me. You left me without giving me a say so. Why did you die? I love you. I hate you for leaving me. I'm so alone, I don't remember the last time I slept and I can't taste food anymore. I want this pain to end, but I need to figure out how. I have no heroes, no friends and no family that's worth the time of day to love or who loves me, except for Tiffany, but she has her own children, so I'm alone. I have no help and no voice. People don't even know how to talk to me. People are nice, like the family I'm staying with. They ask how I'm doing and how do I feel. I tell them that I'm okay or I'm feeling better. They can't handle a real answer though. They don't understand me when I tell them that while my uncle raped my body, I was at the French Open with you watching the Williams sisters play against each other in the final round. They don't understand that sometimes I can smell your polo black cologne and other times I can smell the demons that haunt me. They don't understand that the smell of loneliness, pain, anger, fear, and death overpower me until I need to cut myself to feel alive. You know why, daddy? Because after the tissues are filled with tears and snot, after the casket is closed and, in the ground, after the family has taken everything of value out of the house, Tina is supposed to go back to normal. That's right, Tina is supposed to be happy at family dinners and church. Tina shouldn't talk about not having a daddy to talk about boys, drugs, school or sex. Tina should smile and flip a switch and be everybody's angel. Tina is supposed to hug and be happy after being the pitiful survivor for a couple days. I don't even know who murdered you. There's a person with a face that I cannot see that took you away from me. I refuse to cry about any of the pain or hurt anymore. This world doesn't deserve my tears. I love you daddy and I can't keep living with this hurt, but I refuse to let this world have my tears."

Tina leaned down and placed the letter near the headstone beside five dying roses. Every day for the last month, she wrote a letter to him and placed it on the grave before returning to the foster home. As a cool wind blew by her ear, she believed she could hear her father's voice.

"I can't hear you. Do you remember when we went to the U.S. Open to watch Venus Williams? I was hoping that we could go again next year, after graduation," she said in a warm voice. In her mind, she could communicate with her father if she spoke out loud at the grave site. Feeling alone but feeling like she can hear whispers of her father, she slid down to the grown, lying flat across the grave where fresh grass grew around it. Feeling one with the ground around her Tina inhaled the air around her and exhaled slowly with her eyes closed.

"Grandma isn't doing well. I was living with Aunt Linda and Uncle Daryl. Please don't be mad, but Uncle Daryl molested me and I tried to fight him off, I really did. The police locked him up and they're making me stay with this nice family until I graduate. Aunt Linda sold our house. I don't know what to do, Daddy."

Tina repeated the events that led to her staying at the foster home, feeling that no one else really cared for her and she found solace with speaking to her father's grave, expressing her feelings of sadness and depression.

Overwhelmed with grief over her own situation, she didn't know what else to say. The weight of all that had happened in her short life was too much to bear or talk about. Feeling a lump forming in her throat from the heaviness of recent events, she finally lay still as sleep overcame her.

~~

With no sense of time, Tina woke to the sound of a fire truck's siren blaring in the distant and lifting her head, she could see that the sun was about to set. Looking down at the headstone and placing the new and old letters she wrote together, she suddenly sensed a presence behind her as a whiff of the strong scent of cigar smoke wafted across her nose.

Turning around, she made eye contact with Derrick who pointed a gun at her.

"Give me your money," he shouted with no sign of compassion on his face.

Tina shook nervously as she reached into her pocket and handed him the five-dollar bill she had. While her hand was out, she followed his eyes as he noticed the watch on her arm.

"Give me that watch too," he demanded.

"Please, this is all I have left of my daddy," she begged.

"Give me the watch! Do you want me to kill you

over it?" Derrick screamed pointing the gun closer to her face.

He looked around quickly to be sure no one else was looking before turning back not moved by her plea. He was hoping she wouldn't call his bluff because he knew that the gun wasn't actually loaded. He had a history of robbing and pawning items to survive and he felt that she would be like any other victim. On a normal occasion, he would have shot her and snatched the watch, but today he had an unloaded gun and his prey happened to be in the direction that he walked home.

"Does it matter? Life is a waste of time anyway," she said, unfazed by the gun, feeling that if he shot her, that would actually help bring her close to her father.

"Give me the watch. I don't want to shoot you."

"Here." Tina reached for the watch, snatched it off of her arm and threw it at Derrick's shoes.

Looking in disbelief that she threw the watch at him, Derrick scolds while picking it up and looking at her exposed wrist with cut marks.

"You got problems! Somebody could have really hurt you with that kind of attitude."

"Go to hell," she screamed.

Derrick looked at her arm again and noted the cuts while looking between her face and her arm. He watched as she looked where his eyes had landed and then tried to pull the denim jacket sleeve down.

Derrick thought to himself that she must have been coming to the cemetery to commit suicide. He pondered whether to call the police to get her help before shrugging it off. Having what he wanted, he turned toward the street and ran away.

Tina watched him run away before sighing in disappointment that he didn't question her about the cuts on her wrist that she had made with a razor for the last month just to feel pain and to release tension from the world.

December 8, 2016

"Hey T, I have a question?" Tyrone Clinton said walking up behind Tina who was placing books into her locker at Chester Ridgely High School.

"No," Tina said wanting to be left alone. Over the last few weeks, she tried everything she could to be left alone by everyone in school. Feeling isolated and unable to relate to any of her classmates, she does not understand what Tyrone could want with her.

"I didn't get to ask you the question yet. Can I please ask you this question I really want to ask you and I have wanted to ask you for a while?"

"What?"

"Ok, I've known you since elementary school. I have always liked you and I never knew how to tell you and to be honest, I don't even know if you know my name, but I really wanted to know if you would go to the prom with me?" he asked smiling.

"Your name is Tyrone Clinton and no I can't go to the prom with you," she answered with an angry look on her face and hating herself for what she said because she had always had a crush on him.

"What, why? Coach Eddy said that I can use his car for the prom if I got my grades up. I'm going to be on the honor roll, so we going to be riding there in a BMW."

Not knowing how to tell him that she was living in a foster care shelter for young girls, fearing the backlash from other kids who will figure out she does not have a home to live in and that she does not have any money to buy a prom dress, she decided to end the conversation as fast as possible.

"None of your business," she said, bluntly.

"I really like you. I'm going up the street to the library after school. Can you stay out and study with me? Maybe we can get to know each other," he said, hopeful.

"No. Listen, I like you too, but I can't go to the prom." She didn't want to explain that she had a curfew and that she wanted to check on her grandmother who was recently admitted back into the hospital.

"Well, can I be your boyfriend?" he asked.

Tyrone liked that Tina at least admitted to liking him, too.

"I don't know. You borrowing a cop's car for the prom, you might be snitching."

She smiled devilishly as the conversation lightened.

"He not like the other cops," Tyrone said, chuckling as he walked closer to her, not noticing that she was backing away as he moved in closer.

"None of them can catch my father's killer, so they all the same to me," she said

"I'm sorry about that."

"Don't be. I do want to go to the prom with you, but I might have to transfer soon," she said.

"Ok," Tyrone replied, wondering why Tina would have to transfer schools. "I would go to another school, wait for you to get out and walk you home every day. Just think about it, if you go to another school we will have two proms."

"I hated my life after my dad died, my family sucks, my life sucks. You have been the first person that has been nice to me and haven't done anything to hurt me since my dad died. Well, you and my grandma, but when I need her most, she can't help me."

"I'm sorry about that. I will never hurt you and I will always be with you." He reached out and took Tina by the hand.

"I want you to have something," Tina said moving her hand from his and reaching back into her locker. She pulled out a signed picture of Serena and Venus Williams playing tennis. "My dad took me to see them play each other at the U.S. Open. They signed this for me. It's the only thing I have that I value in this world and I want you to have it to remember me by when

I'm not with you."

"Ok," Tyrone said and took the picture from her.

~~

Walking past the old Ridgely Marketplace, an area where several prostitutes commonly congregate to solicit drivers, Tina reached into her pocket, grabbed a handful of pills she took from her grandmother's hospital room. Thinking momentarily about the failing circle of support in her life, including her dislike for the hospital's social worker, she laughed at the idea that Tyrone would have been any better than anyone else that had let her down when she needed them.

After failing to swallow the pills without anything to drink, she walked into a Garland and Son Auto Parts Store and purchased a bottle of water. The store has served the Ridgley Square Community for more than forty years. After swallowing the remainder of the pills, she asked the clerk if she could use the bathroom. Knowing it is against store policy for non-staff members to use the restroom, he looked around to be sure no one was paying them any attention.

"Yes," he said, thinking that it would cause no harm to help. He walked her toward the back of the store.

Locking the door behind her and feeling dizzy, Tina collapsed to the floor as visions of father and daughter dances, family dinners and tennis games flood her mind. The room began to stop spinning as time froze and she heard her father's deep baritone voice.

"This is a rook," the voice said as a hand showed the movement of the large wooden chess piece. "This is the bishop and this is the king," the voice continued as more wooden chess pieces appeared on the wooden chess board. "The king can only move one place at a time, so you have to protect it at all times. You have to be on defense to protect the king. This is the queen," the voice informed as a wooden hand-carved chess piece is placed on the board. "She runs the board, some would say she is the most powerful piece. That's probably why there's only one, like you."

As the pieces to the chessboard disappeared, the voice faded off into the darkness as a young child with pigtails and a tall dark-skinned male drank out of a small toy tea set at the park. "You shouldn't be here," a strong, deep baritone familiar voice said to the child as a strong emotional cloud of disappointment and sadness overcame Tina.

"You shouldn't either," the child, that appeared to be a younger form of her said back as she sipped out of the toy tea cup. "It sucks back there."

"I know. I didn't want you to come here yet. Time is not a relevant thing here. All we have is time to reflect and wait on judgement. You had a whole life to build memories and you wasted it. Why?" the larger than life male that appeared to be a form of Laurence said.

"What was I supposed to do?" she questioned as everything turned black and she saw Tiffany walking into the viewing room with tears in her eyes.

"I'm so sorry," Tiffany apologized over the plastic coffin, feeling that this day had become a gauntlet of grief. "You didn't deserve this, I should have done something about my dad when I had the chance."

"You knew your father was a rapist and you did nothing," the voice said in anger.

"Please forgive me," Tiffany pleaded looking back as her son Darrin walked through the door of the viewing room. "I told my momma several times in the past and she told me to shut up. Uncle Leon and Uncle Larry took care of it. I never thought that my dad would do it again, especially to you. Grandma gave me the chance to do something a few months ago, and I didn't."

"They knew about him, too?" the voice questioned as the woman next to the fireplace said, "Tiffany."

"Who are you?" Tiffany asked turning around to the frail woman.

"Gina."

"Tina's teacher?" Tiffany asked.

"No, her mother. I've been clean for two months. I heard about what happened to Larry and I've been trying to find Tina.".

"You're not my mother!" the voice screeches. "My mother is dead. Dead, you hear me!"

"So, you were trying to find her to get custody?"

"No, I came to make amends for things I have done wrong in the past."

"So, you come to your daughter's funeral to make

amends? Drugs must really rot your brain," Tiffany said.

Not being able to stand the conversation anymore, she walked out of the chapel, grabbed her son by the arm and escorted him out into the funeral home's hallway. She released his hand and noticed her own mother, Linda, standing outside of the Gardenia Chapel. "You weren't much better."

"Excuse me?" Linda said, caught off guard by the remark, as her grandchild hugged her waist.

"You let daddy do that to me, you let him get away with it and he did the same thing to Tina. You're no better than Gina," she blurted out.

"Who?" Linda questioned.

"Tina's mom. She's in there with Tina."

"No, she's not!" Linda fiercely declared walking to The Monte Cassino Chapel.

"It doesn't matter. You're no better than her. Both of y'all failed your kids."

"I get that you're upset. There is a lot going on. Your child Kenya, your grandmother, your ex Keyon and your little cousin Tina are all here. I have my problems, that is true, but your grandmother wouldn't want this, not here. Come by my place tonight. There's something I need to talk to you about."

"What?" Tiffany yells in anger.

"Your grandmother left her house to you in the will. She didn't want Titan to throw you and your kids out on the street," Linda said as she walked toward the

Monte Cassino Chapel. Inside, a faint voice began to whisper.

"You were never my mother. You weren't there for me, for daddy, for anybody. This is just as much your fault as it was Uncle Daryl's."

Walking out of the viewing room, Gina avoided eye contact with Linda as she glanced at the Protea viewing room. After reading the name, Simon Little, she attempted to remember where she knew that name. After thinking about conversations with an old friend, she yelled, "Silk!"

Unbeknownst to Gina, Anna Cartwright walked by with curiosity.

"Who is Silk?" she asked.

Anna was eager to have a new developing story after the Tyrone Clinton protest ended. She and her media crew recently left the Orchard Chapel observing the crowd of protesters and advocates.

"Simon Little," Gina responded. "He had a sex change a few years ago and went by the name Silk Diamond. She used to work for the radio station. Her parents were rich and a lot of people knew who they were. They are Sedrick and Erica Little."

"I know the Little family very well."

Anna pulled out her cell phone to send a text message to her cameraman.

"How did she die?" Gina asked dealing with the shock of her friend's death. She looked as Anna showed her a picture of Silk Diamond on her phone.

"They found her body about two weeks ago."

Anna showed Gina a picture on her phone of Simon Little inside of the coffin. The Bradley Funeral Home began placing pictures on their website of the deceased in the coffin as a way to connect family members that could not attend viewings or wake services.

"That's her," Gina screamed.

"Come with me," Anna stated, spotting her camera crew in the hallway exiting the Orchard Chapel.

7
THE IRIS CHAPEL

Inside of the Bradley Funeral Home's largest chapel, a black plastic and gold casket sits in the front near the pulpit. Surrounded by several flowers, cards, pictures and a poster with several signatures, the coffin was draped with an American flag.

"It's empty in here," a voice whispered softly in the hollow viewing room. "I can see I was loved," the voice said in reflection to the flowers and cards. "I just wish someone was here for me."

April 17, 2006

"Michelle was my wife," Pastor Donald Avery said to his filled to capacity church, as he glanced at the beautiful wood coffin. "I won't sugar coat our past because we both used heroin in the past and were addicts. We spent close to two hundred dollars a night getting high until she found God. I didn't have any interest in church. All I saw was a white man with blue eyes and blonde hair brainwashing black people to worship him. Then I saw the change in the woman that would later become my wife. She stopped using and got a job." Pausing for a second, he noticed his wife's parents and other family members. "She then started to ask about getting married because she didn't want to live in sin anymore. I didn't know what she was talking about, but I loved her. I started marriage counseling with her pastor and before long, I got clean and got saved myself. Michelle was always a guiding light and a ray of hope."

Glancing down at the coffin, Pastor Avery held back his tears.

"You know, I've preached a lot of funerals for church members, friends and strangers. It's weird doing one for someone you shared many intimate moments with. We had and achieved a lot of dreams together. I remember when she said she wanted to go back to school for addictions counseling. There were lots of late nights of her studying and doing papers. When she walked across that stage to get her bachelor's degree, you would have thought God himself had given her a million dollars."

As the church began to chuckle at his comment, he thought back to the day she graduated from college. He thought about the money they donated to the institution and the fact that the doors are now closed to that small college due to a complication with their accreditation.

"At a certain time, you begin to think about legacy. Hers was always reaching back to bring people forward, like the Sankofa bird, that symbolizes going back to your roots in order to move forward. The thing that hurts is she reached back too far. I'm sure many of you heard the rumors and they are true. My wife did relapse and she died of an overdose."

As many of the members gasped, Pastor Avery looked on at various facial expressions.

"Make no mistake, the wages of the sin, is always death. While we will all go this way, until the Lord's return, we have a choice in how we can and will live. I, nor you, have a place to judge my wife's life. What I do have are memories, but that does not get her into heaven or hell. Today, I am charged with reminding you that your next sin could be your last sin and that could be the blemish that keeps you out of the kingdom. We all have to live a drop dead ready lifestyle. If I die in this moment or the next, does it gratify God? Will that moment be the reason I miss the kingdom of God? The word of God talks about the story of the ten virgins, five were wise, had oil for the bridegroom. Five were foolish, did not have oil and had to go get some. During that time, they had to go get the oil and they missed the coming of the bridegroom. Instances and moments happen around here that could be our last every day and we have to be drop dead ready because we don't know when our last day on this earth is. My wife's book has come to a close. How will you write your next chapter?"

January 17, 2016

"Brother Edward, I wanted to talk to you about something," Pastor Avery said as Edward Carter stood on the top stone step outside of the church.

"How can I help?" Edward asked.

"I see your passion for coaching sports at the high school and you are always doing something great in this community. You are one of the most respected police officers in the city. How would you like to become a member on our deacon board?"

"I would love to," Edward said shaking the pastor's hand. "I would really love to join the deacon board. I wanted to talk to you about something else."

"How can I help?" Pastor Avery asked while feeling a sharp pain in his stomach?

Revealing a small black box, he showed the pastor a beautiful engagement ring.

"I want to marry Sister Ciara. I want to pop the question on our anniversary in a few months, would you mind praying for me, so that I know I'm making the right decision?"

May 16, 2016

"There's a lot of promise in this district," Pastor Avery said inside of the community association meeting as the Little and Titan families sat prominently in front of a group of onlookers. "Mother Florence Simms has served as the chair of this association for over twenty years and helped us through some tough times, but we never lost who we were. Who we were was a family and a village united. We turn out for these kids' proms, we support them in graduations, we raised them in daycare and we watched them play sports and games. We see them date, have kids, get jobs and become something. We hear the marching bands and the step teams. We have seen some die, get locked up and come home. In all of that, we are all together. To offer any of us a dime to give that up and destroy our culture, our community, our homes is traitorous."

He paused for a brief moment while experiencing pain in his side. He searched for and found Amber Sage, owner of Sage Reality.

"It shouldn't be a question. My church was the only theater in the city where blacks could go and feel human during the civil rights era. Adrian, your grandfather and mother ran domino and card tournaments every weekend which helped put food on some of y'all's tables."

He looked to other familiar faces.

"Randy, your grandmother had rent parties almost every other weekend and that's how a lot of you all kept your bills paid. Ms. Paulette, I remember your great grandmother used to own that corner unit across the street. That was a juke joint for all of us and Vanessa's mother use to sing there."

He paused again when he began to feel nauseous. "The point I'm getting at is this is our home, our community. The only reason those developers want to buy us out of here is because they see the promise that we already have."

"You are talking about yesterday, we're talking about money right now," Chanel said as a group of young people laughed.

"No," Minister Hakeem uttered while standing in solidarity with Pastor Avery. "What he is talking about is yesterday, today and tomorrow. We had greatness in this district. We have problems in our district today and we can build for greatness tomorrow without you pushing us out."

"Do you realize that's seventy stacks you're talking about throwing away?" a young man in the crowd of people yelled.

"Your grandmother had that house," Minister Hakeem scolded back. "Your mother had it and now you and your son have it. Where will you go if you move with your seventy thousand? Is your credit good enough to live in the county? Are you ready to rent and pay that every month? Last time I checked, that house has been paid off for forty years. You take that money and you're walking into something uncertain. You turn that money down, you still have a house that you pay the lights and taxes on."

"I could really use that money," the young man responded back.

"Where?" Pastor Avery asked.

"I could get the same car that cop got," he said.

"Where would you park it at?" Edward Carter asked, knowing the reference was made to the BMW he drove.

"I don't know. Maybe my new apartment."

"So, you go from a house that you only pay the light bill for to a hypothetical apartment?" Edward asked shaking his head. "You do know if we build this area up, the houses will be worth more than seventy thousand, right?"

"But I can buy a BMW."

"You understand you can buy one with a job?" Minister Hakeem interjects shaking his head. "No disrespect to Officer Carter, but his car decreased in value as soon as he purchased it and drove it off the lot. In all honesty, if he paid seventy thousand for the car, it might not be worth forty grand today, but your grandmother's house could be worth over a hundred thousand this time next year."

"Let's focus on what we really have instead of maybe's," Chandler said with a smile. "You can get up to seventy thousand today by signing the property over to us."

July 23, 2016

"We don't have it in the budget to keep paying for Brother Keyon," Mother Simms informed Pastor Avery as the two sat inside of his office. "None of the trustees have a problem with him living at the church. Paying for him to work the grounds and take care of the maintenance is too much of a weight for the church. We're over budget as it is and too many families are leaving the church. Jobs are moving out of the city and we just don't have it," she explained.

"We need to have it," Pastor Avery said looking at the minutes from the last church meeting. "Keyon has a new job at the warehouse and he already told me that he will be moving into his new apartment soon. That's an expense we don't have to worry about."

"You helped the other child, Allen, with money we didn't have."

"It was necessary," Pastor Avery replied looking at the financial report. "We have to do our part to birth ministries."

"We can't afford it," she declared leaning back in the chair. "We're going to lose this property. We have been behind on payments and we won't be able to pay this property off in time. Do you remember the contract we signed with Sage for this rent-to-own?"

"Yes," Pastor Avery answered. He thought about some of the bad decisions he'd made and some of the good choices he's made, too.

"You know Brother Allen is a repeat offender, right? That money you put into him could be gone. Will you bail him out of jail, too?"

"Mother Simms, when your granddaughter, Tiffany, was behind on her rent, you came to the church asking us to help. We did and didn't ask any questions. Tiffany has had baby after baby and we did not judge or condemn her. When she didn't have the food for those children, we helped without a discussion. Why is it a problem for Keyon, Kenya's father, to earn an honest income here? Why is it a problem for us to give him a second chance when the church has run out of fingers to count the chances Tiffany has had?"

"Excuse me, but that day, that young man went to my granddaughter's house looking for trouble."

"He was trying to see his daughter. If Tiffany was not shacking up with that man, this situation would not have happened," Pastor Avery said.

Trying not to grow angry, he let his mind drift to his previous chemotherapy appointment. Feeling that he should have disclosed to the church's staff that he has been battling hepatitis C and pancreatic cancer for the last few years, he heard Mother Simms repeating herself.

"Are you trying to say that the situation was my granddaughter's fault?"

"Sin created the situation," Pastor Avery professed as he thought about his own past and what led to his Hepatitis C and late stage cancer diagnoses.

He reminisced on his drug usage during the Vietnam War and using when he returned to America. He now appreciated life for not being worse, such as not contracting HIV when he shared needles with people while using heroin. He also remembered the day he heard that his wife overdosed inside of a vacant house. He thought about who would take over the church and what kind of shape would he leave the church in if he died from his bout with the dual diagnosis. "We all have the choice to sin or to avoid sin. Your daughter sinned by having sex before marriage and brother Keyon sinned by having sex before marriage and fighting that young man. That young man sinned by fighting Keyon."

"So, what's your point in all of this?" she asked.

"I see each one of the people in this church being a part of the ministry. We can reach more people doing what we are naturally good at. If we have patience and trust God, we can pay this property off. Sage Realty has been patient with us and denied all of the offers that Titan has made."

"You're a fool. Not one ministry can operate if we do not keep the doors to this church open. What are you going to do, have the usher board march down North Avenue? Are you going to have the missionary department hand out water and coats to the homeless every day? Are you going to have the trustees count money on Hilton Avenue? You need this building to do anything. Stop being foolish."

Mother Simms had had enough and stood to leave.

July 26, 2016

"How is everything coming along?" Pastor Avery asked Keyon as he worked on a circuit breaker.

"This thing is a little dated. You grab anything to

eat yet?"

"No."

"Do you like Pizza?"

"Yes, I do."

"Want to go to Jerry's?"

"I would love to."

"My treat," Keyon said. "I have some great news."

"What's that?" Pastor Avery asked as they walked toward the door exiting the church.

"I was approved to move into the apartment up the street and they hired me on a part-time basis to work in their Heating, Ventilation and Air Conditioning Department."

"I'm glad to hear that," the pastor said as a car ran the red light. "It's really a shame how people don't regard human life."

September 26, 2016

"So, you're not going to pay my lawyer's retainer fee?" Daryl asked Linda as she sat across the visiting room table from him, next to Pastor Avery. The trio were seated inside of the classroom sized visiting room at the Maryland Correctional Institution in Jessup which is also commonly known as MCI-J. The institution frequently housed parole and probation violators with their regular prison population of medium and maximum-security level inmates. Dressed in denim pants and a blue button up shirt, Daryl was annoyed that his wife brought her former pastor into their personal business.

"No. Why did you have to do that to Tina?" she asked in a low voice as Pastor Avery clutched her hand, knowing that his role is to support her during the challenges she has had with Daryl.

"What?" he shouted emphatically, glancing around the room at other groups of inmates and visitors having personal conversations. "You bring him down here to ask about what happens in our home?"

"I don't come here to judge," Pastor Avery said in a calm voice.

"You should have judged the affairs of your church as much as you judge my family," Daryl muttered, leaning back in the chair. "You lost your church due to money, so what, you milking my wife for money now? That's why you can't pay my lawyer, Linda? You paying this church pimp?"

"No, I'm tired of you doing what you been doing to these girls. Your own daughter was beautiful and innocent and I can't even say the things you did to her for years and then Tina," she said.

"Don't sit here in front of this pastor acting like you're without fault here," Daryl said. "What are you talking about? You're as much at fault as I am," Daryl declared.

Neither noticed Pastor Avery as he grabbed at his side in pain.

"You covered for me for all those years, making excuses for what I did. The way I see it, you're just as guilty as I am. Hell, the way I see it, they need to put you in the cell I'm in."

"That's uncalled for," Pastor Avery said, though he felt nauseous and lightheaded.

"Why are you here?" Daryl asked.

"Where's the car?" Linda asked. Somehow, her husband's car mysteriously disappeared. She never did believe the story that it had been stolen.

"Linda, it's been gone since August. Like I said to the police that day, somebody stole it."

"I didn't believe it then and I don't believe it now."

"I'm already in jail, so does the truth really matter at this point?" he mockingly pointed out, walking to the back area before stopping and turning back around. "You still have to live with the guilt of the part you played. I know who I am, but you don't know who you are. False Prophet Avery, here, can't change what you allowed to happen with your own flesh and blood."

Standing up and walking to the exit of the visiting room, Pastor Avery looked away from the reinforced glass and metal door toward Linda.

"You have to do better." Confused by his comment, Linda looked back in question as he continued. "Your husband is in prison for something that could have been avoided years ago, if you would have reported him for what he did to your daughter."

"This is not your place," Linda replied in a low voice, trying not to be noticed by other visitors as the door to the visiting room opened and a correctional officer escorted the two into the bright and well-kept lobby area of the prison.

"Actually, it is. Your mother is having the fight of her life with her health, your daughter has alienated you with her children and your husband is in prison. How much further down do you have to go before you get the message that's being told to you. You have protected that husband of yours for too long and everything has gotten away from you while he has done no good for you."

"Thank you, Pastor," she sarcastically interjected.

"Don't thank me yet. I came here to support you and I'm trying. With addiction, we use and relapse constantly. The idea of sobriety normally doesn't stick until you hit rock bottom which is that moment you have burned every bridge with family, shelters, friends, jobs, anything you can think of. At that moment of rock bottom, you have a solemn moment between you and God. It's very intimate and scary because you know you messed up and you're about to die alone if you continue. You're almost right there at rock bottom and if you don't get it together soon, you're going to hit that ground hard and it's going to hurt. When I was using, it was easy to get high and if I didn't have the money, I knew who did or where to get it from. The hardest thing I had to do was try to do better for myself, but it was worth it when I did. It's time you do the hard thing and let your drug of choice go."

"I don't do any drugs," Linda answered as he shook his head.

"Daryl is your drug, Linda. You're so addicted to having a man love you that you don't realize this isn't love. You love him, but you're being abused, used and taken advantage of. You're losing everything around you for a man that is happy to take from you and keep taking until you die from him. Ask your niece, Tina."

"I tried to help her," Linda answered.

"You meant well, but the road to hell is paved with good intentions. You knew as soon as you let her in the house that you were leading her to slaughter with Daryl. You can deny it, but deep down you knew he would do the same to her as he did to Tiffany. You don't have to allow it to happen any longer. Secretly, you wanted to have this talk which is why you brought me here to support you, am I right?"

"You are, but I didn't want to hurt Tina. She lost everything and she needed her family. Daryl isn't a bad person, he just needs help."

"Sometimes, you have to let the professionals help those in need and you stay in the lane that you're good in," Pastor Avery said unlocking and opening the passenger door to his champagne colored Lincoln Continental for Linda to get in.

December 16, 2016

"There were some of your friends from the Veterans

Administration Hospital here to see you today," Allen Bradley said walking over to the black and gold casket.

"Thank you," he said examining the flowers. "Actually, thank you is not enough. I really appreciate that you paid for me to go to college."

Allen walked over to a picture of a young Donald Avery wearing his United States Army Class A uniform in front of the American flag.

"You believed in me and because of your input, I was able to become a mortician. I used some of the money you gave me along with a grant to open this funeral home. I could have come to church more often and for that I'm sorry, pastor."

Allen walked back over to the casket and placed his hand near the top as he spoke.

"I should not have made myself so busy with everything going on. I did pay my tithes to Mother Simms. I didn't know she had Alzheimer's until she was on her way out. It hurts worse to know what was happening to the church."

Glancing back at the door to the chapel, Allen noticed people walking into other viewing rooms but no one had entered into the Iris Chapel.

"Edward, Ciara and I were working together for the community center that was just opened. Keyon and I were talking about him teaching a heating, ventilation and air conditioning and carpentry class before he died in the car accident. Silk, who used to stop into the church here and there was found dead almost two weeks ago. It's sad what happened to her. You'd never guess who her parents are."

Allen patted his hand on the coffin near the top of the American Flag.

"I don't know if you heard about Mother Simms' granddaughter before you passed, but Tina took her life a day or two before she passed away. After that, we created a group at the center for survivors of sexual trauma. Ciara has been helping us open a shelter for some of the people that do not have a safe place to stay."

Walking to one of the front pew seats and sitting down, Allen looked up at the casket.

"I still remember one of the messages you preached years ago. It helped me turn my life over to Jesus. It was titled '*Between the Dash*'. You remember that?"

"There is a time for everything and a season for every activity under the heavens," a voice whispered as Allen sat on the pew looking at the coffin.

"You preached about what you have to do with your time and that helped me. That was the moment when I really heard God's voice. That same Sunday, I had a thirty-eight tucked under my shirt and a bag of weed in my pocket. You preached that message and I threw it away in the trash can in the fellowship hall."

Allen could feel tears falling down his cheeks as he talked through memories.

"I named each one of these viewing rooms after a flower. I believe that each person that comes in here plants a seed and that the people that come in and out are what bloomed from the person's life in the viewing room. The irony to that statement is, in here is just you and me. Yet today, I have a full funeral home with people that you have impacted in some way, shape or form. Silk, Deacon Carter, Keyon, Kenya, Tina and Mother Simms all have funerals today."

Allen thought about the irony in naming each room after a flower and almost each person was an extension of Pastor Avery.

"It's like the whole church was raptured together," he joked. "Even though each of these people are gone, they left hope for the future. Linda agreed to pay off the church's debt with Sage Reality using Mother Simms life insurance policy along with the tithe money that she forgot to turn in. Minister Hakeem Andrews has agreed to help pastor the church until we can fill the position. He said that it will not slow him down from finishing his dissertation. I told him that we need someone as engaged with the community and dedicated to making an overall difference as you were."

Feeling a warm hand touch his shoulder, Allen glanced back to see Minister Hakeem's face with a nod of approval. He watched him walk toward the pulpit.

"I find it amazing that cameras can follow around so much negativity. They can watch us kill us or dance and belittle one another, but not one news story about the impact this man had on people's lives has been done."

Hakeem glanced at Allen observing a picture directly in front of him as community and former church members of New Hope Greater Love Church enter the chapel and took seats. The viewing room began to fill up as Hakeem removed the microphone from the stand and held it. Hakeem has long hated speaking behind a podium and preferred to walk and talk.

"I just left out of a packed viewing room two doors down for a black teenager killed by police during a robbery. That gains ratings for the news, so they are in there, probably looking for a riot. In the same funeral home, we have a cop who was killed for trying to be there for a child that was shot by another cop. The media doesn't spin that cop's involvement in the community. No, they talk about him being the victim of angry black people. This man lying here helped to open the doors to this funeral home, a place that has created programs to keep people alive in this community. The media may cover a small portion of a story to a great audience, but we celebrate the works of this man."

He smiles at the sound of applause.

"He may not be with us any longer, but his works, efforts and vision does not have to stop. Dr. Martin Luther King once preached a sermon that said *'If I Had Sneezed.'* In that sermon he talked about a knife almost puncturing his artery and if he had sneezed he would have drowned in his own blood, preventing him from doing all the good works that he had accomplished in life. In this community we are stabbed constantly with crime, drugs, and poverty, but we don't have to sneeze. We don't have to inherit other challenges of being infected by viruses that will stop us from achieving our greatness and promise. That includes falling into the cycle of addiction, not having wealth, creating debt, not being self-sufficient, dropping out of school or falling into the trap of the criminal justice system. This is what Pastor Avery stood up against."

Making eye contact with Erica and Sedrick Little as they entered the chapel, he noticed Chanel and Chandler Titan and directed his next statement at them.

"It's up to us to care about, rebuild and reshape this community. We have the power to be the change this community needs, individually and collectively. Today we mourn this man, tomorrow we hurt, but every day we have the choice to keep his legacy alive. That legacy was for us to make a difference, to make an impact and to build a future, here. It doesn't matter how hard or impossible it may seem, no matter what challenges may come, we fight, we build, we grow, together."

Walking toward the Iris Chapel with a camera crew, Anna Cartwright and Gina approach the Titan and Little families as they stood at the rear door of the viewing room.

"Is it true you all have been covering up Silk Diamond's death?" Anna asked in a forceful tone to Erica Little.

"Excuse me?" Erica responded as Chandler glanced back at Anna and sighed because he was familiar with her antics and desire for television drama.

"I'm talking about the fact that your daughter, Silk Diamond's, body was discovered two weeks ago and had a funeral service today. A specific group of people were invited as guests to her funeral. She was known as Silk Diamond, the transgender radio personality. I learned of this when one of her friends noticed Silk's name on the chapel door. Why have you hidden this from the public?"

"What are you saying I've hidden from the public?" Sedrick asked angrily while trying to avoid the question as a large crowd of people look on from the Iris Chapel.

"Mr. Little, your daughter was murdered and missing for months and was recently discovered, yet you held a community meeting at a senior center a few months ago saying your child had been dead a few months. Did you have knowledge of her death then?"

"No," Sedrick answer while glancing at Chanel and Chandler Titan.

"With the work that you are doing in the Ridgely Square Community, are you really trying to segregate the proposed project from the Lesbian-Gay-Bisexual-

Transgender-Queer community?" Anna asked.

Chandler stepped in front of the camera.

"Pardon me, but in no way, shape or form are we trying to segregate anyone," he said.

"Then why have your business partners alienated themselves from their own transgender son?" Anna asked.

"No one had knowledge of Simon's death," Erica said as the Titans tried to walk away.

"Then why did you say your son was dead at the community meeting?" Anna continued. "If this is the kind of community that you are building, this does not seem like it has the community's best interest at heart. Tell us, are there other people that you're trying to segregate like African Americans, Asian Americans, Latino Americans, Middle Easterners?"

"We are not segregating anyone," Chanel yelled as everyone in the Iris Chapel looked toward the rear.

"We had no knowledge of the Littles' transgender son or his funeral today, but we will look into why this has happened," Chandler aggressively stated as his sister sat down in the back row of the viewing room.

"We covered it up," Sedrick said as Anna's eyes opened wide. "You see, my wife learned of our son's whereabouts from a private investigator and she found him at a shelter."

"Why do you keep calling Silk Diamond a him?" Gina asked. "She had a legal sex change. Everybody in this city knows who she was. She was a radio legend here. Please be respectful to my friend."

"Simon was staying at a shelter when my wife found him. We then lost contact with him until we had to identify his body," Sedrick said giving Gina a repulsive look.

"Did you accept Silk's sexuality?" Anna asked.

"No. It was a sin and an abomination. The wages of sin is death and he is dead for his choices. That's why I had him cremated as a man," Sedrick responded.

"Is that why you hid Silk's death and funeral from everyone in Baltimore?" Gina asked as Anna smiled, admiring how well her newfound friend handled this situation?

"It's an embarrassment to my family. We chose not to have anyone like that around us, even if it is our own child," Sedrick answered as Erica walked away from everyone and headed toward the exit of the funeral home.

"Well then, we choose not to have your company in our district if your views are that hateful to other human beings," Minister Hakeem said walking behind Sedrick.

"I don't believe that this is the best place to discuss business, but we are pulling our offer away from this district until we can come to terms as business partners," Chanel said walking back toward Chandler and Sedrick hoping to get her colleagues attention to leave the growing fiasco.

"Gina, how would you feel about working for me? I

would like to run a piece on community affairs and I think you would do great in that department. I wouldn't mind starting out running a documentary on your life, if you're open to that," Anna said as her cameraman motioned that he had stopped recording.

"I'm willing to try. I actually received a bachelor's degree in journalism many moons ago. I met my late husband in college where he was studying to be a teacher and I wanted to do news broadcasting," Gina said as Minister Hakeem and Councilman Dawson walked throughout the chapel shaking hands with visitors.

Turning around and looking at all of the people inside the large viewing area, Allen turned to the coffin.

"I know that you can't smell the flowers that the people left, but please know that the seeds that you have planted in everyone's lives have bloomed into something beautiful."

8
EPILOGUE

Who will take up the mantel after the race ends for those before us? This was a question asked in various ways by many people, some not ready for the question or the answer.

Florence Simms, the matriarch of the family, took on many loads, including being the silent voice of reason leading the family reunion and being the backbone of her church. Out of all of her children, she was always let down by Linda, but made constant attempts to push her in the right direction. She felt that Daryl preyed on Linda's naïveté and free spirit. She learned that Daryl molested Tiffany and began to support her granddaughter. Florence had a keen eye for Linda's engagement with Daryl and Tiffany and admired Tiffany's strength as a care giver, nurturer and strong voice. She placed Tiffany into her will because she realized Tiffany had the best skills to maintain the family house and keep it in the family's name.

Leon and his household lived in a different state with no interest in returning and Laurence, of course, had been murdered while Linda showed that she could not handle responsibility.

Sasha continued to work at the hospital and engaged in grief support groups. Eventually, she found a mutual friend, Tiffany Gibbons, whom she could bond with over the death of her child and the struggles of living on fixed income.

Titan Industries continued their plan to close the apartment complex, which caused Sasha to become temporarily homeless until Tiffany welcomed her into her house with open arms.

Sasha participated in a documentary produced by Anna Cartwright that followed the lives of African American mothers who lost their children to police involved shootings. Following the airing of the show, Anna published a book on her life and the hardships she faced. The autobiography led to the production of a motion picture which inspired Sasha to continue working as an author.

Chanel and Chandler Titan continued developing communities in different east coast cities. They have been actively negotiating with Baltimore City for the Ridgely Square Community, but they agreed to halt business dealings with Erica and Sedrick Little.

The Littles went on to participate in grief and couples counseling after the business separation with Titan Industries. Erica felt that Sedrick did not provide strong enough support in her decision to isolate Silk and decided to file for divorce. The two have had a lengthy divorce proceeding due to Erica's desire to obtain some control of Grand Regal Suites.

Ciara and Allen began dating a few months after working on the funeral home's community project. They were married a year after and gave birth to two sons, Carter and Edward.

Trish, the social worker, is still employed at the hospital and the treatment center. She recently faced another financial crisis due to wage garnishment.

Daryl 'Cube' Gibbons was released from prison due to a technicality in Tina's case and has been missing for two years.

Tiffany broke up with Tony three weeks after her daughter, grandmother and cousin's funerals. She graduated with a Bachelor's of Science in Nursing and obtained a Master's degree in Public Health at Morgan State University. She is now a Project and Facilities Coordinator at Ridgely Square Hospital.

Tiffany and Sasha worked together to create a not-for-profit organization to provide support for women and young girls who experienced sexually traumatic situations.

Tiffany and Minister Hakeem Andrews are now engaged to be married and have reopened the New Hope Greater Love Church where he now presides as pastor.

Linda moved to Arizona with Leon to start her life over. Since her migration to the west coast, she gained a job as a tax preparer and filed for divorce from

Daryl. The divorce is still pending since Daryl remains a missing person.

A NOTE FROM THE AUTHOR

The idea of *The Wake* was to touch on various topics in Baltimore City that include gentrification, substance abuse and food desert, which is a home that is a mile or further away from an affordable source of fresh vegetables, fruits or meats. Other topics include police and community relations, molestation, health disparities, family secrets and complicated grief. As a licensed clinician who provides case management, crisis interventions, grief counseling and mental health therapy on a daily basis, the stories in this book can easily come to life, though are written as fictional accounts. All of the areas of Ridgley Square were inspired by real Baltimore City locations.

The story of the Gibbons and Simms families explored the dynamic of covering up a family secret, such as child molestation and how the secret affected Tina after Tiffany learned to cope and avoid the abuse.

Daryl's behavior may have stemmed from possible Dissociative Identity Disorder, which may have also led to his uncontrolled impulses around women or his development after experiencing sexual trauma as a child.

Linda identified the need for having an ideal family after watching her mother, Florence Simms, raise she and her brothers with only the support of her uncle. The effects of the poor relationship Linda had with Daryl created a direct problem with Tiffany and her desire to have relationships with men for short periods of time before isolating herself.

Florence's health problems were related to her poor diet since the Ridgley Square community did not have convenient access to grocery stores and a lot of food purchased was processed, which created health challenges for her health.

Tina's death was an illustration of complicated grief which included being raped by her uncle after the murder of her father. Her mother, Gina, left the home at an early age with an addiction to crack cocaine and heroin. She began sex work to manage her substance addiction. Not having the benefit of living with her support system which included Tiffany, Florence, Pastor Avery or Linda, following the sexual assault that occurred and a bad assessment in the emergency room, Tina's complicated grief evolved into Post-Traumatic-Stress and Major Depression.

The Post Traumatic Stress Disorder was presented when Tina felt uncomfortable around Tyrone at the locker, attempting to move away from him while he spoke. The major depression, induced by the sexual assault and contracting HIV, included cutting herself, writing daily notes to her deceased father, sleeping on his grave and eventually taking her own life.

Edward Carter's longing to improve the police

department's community relationship was due to his attachment to Ridgley Square. Officer Carter had grown up in the community, attended school, church and coached football in the area. He truly believed his involvement in the community made a difference and other police officers should have similar motivations to make Baltimore City more than a place that an officer works. Edward and Hakeem both understood the importance of investing in Baltimore and the need to earn and spend money in Baltimore City to improve the schools, roads, and community. Edward believed that if the police department's relationship with the community was better, than his star player, Tyrone Clinton, would not have experienced a lethal use of force.

Sedrick and Erica Little experienced complicated grief by their ability to cope with the remembrance of Silk. Erica's experience with Silk was a constant reminder of her deceased daughter Sabrina. Silk believed that Sabrina lived in her head and controlled a lot of her behaviors. Silk and Sabrina were twins and Silk witnessed the death of Sabrina in traffic which created a lasting trauma. Silk's lifestyle was not accepted by Sedrick and Erica and created barriers to how they would think of her, even the idea of public perception was troubling to the couple. It was easier to cremate Silk and keep the death private, than to have a remembrance ceremony. The family isolated Silk to the point, that she was dead to them prior to having knowledge that she was murdered. Before fully being able to mourn and move forward with the death of Silk, in the image they would want to accept, the public discovered that Silk was dead at the funeral home, by coincidence of another unrelated funeral taking place. This created a compound problem of the community remembering who Silk was, the Littles' business deal and trying to maintain an image of a prestigious family.

ABOUT THE AUTHOR

Kyle Berkley is a husband and father from Baltimore, Maryland. He completed his education in Baltimore City public schools and graduated from Frederick Douglass High School.

Kyle attended Coppin State College with a major in history. He then continued his education at Sojourner Douglass College and Morgan State University, where he earned his Bachelor's and Master's Degrees in Social Work.

Kyle and his wife, Rebecca, created a nonprofit organization called the *4 Us Initiative,* providing safe housing for homeless families, victims of domestic violence and preventive care for adolescents.

From 1998 until 2013, Kyle wrote and produced music for various music groups, such as Dogg University, R-Sinal Records and Funk out the Trunk. He was a radio personality, along with Eri Carter, for Open Mic Radio.

In 2014, Kyle was elected as a representative to the Baltimore City State Central Committee. He also provided mental health therapy, grief counseling and case management at several Baltimore City shelters, hospitals, transitional houses, outpatient medical, crisis response teams and substance abuse treatment centers. Kyle is currently earning his Ph. D at Walden University and can be reached on social media outlets, Facebook, Twitter and Instagram at *Berkley4Us*.

The website for the *4 Us Initiative* is
http://www.4usinitiative.org

ABOUT THE PUBLISHER

Cheryl Barton Publishing, LLC is a book publishing company dedicated to helping writers become authors. Our foundation is based on the belief that there is a writer in all of us and there are people who would love to read what we all have to say. Our company motto is, *"We're Turning Writers into Authors"*.

Our CEO, Cheryl Barton, is a published author who has written and self-published over twenty-five novels. She has also published books by several other authors. She brings all that she has learned in writing and publishing to the table when it comes to helping other writers fulfill their dreams.

For more information about the services provided by Cheryl Barton Publishing and to see other book selections, visit our website at www.crbarton.com.